Suddenly, out of the corner of the policeman's eye, he saw motion where there shouldn't have been any. "What the hell?" he started to say, when flame leaped out of the darkness. A hard blow hit him in the chest and he staggered heavily. As he reeled back against the car, the night seemed to explode with fire. He clawed at his holster, but it was a feeble effort. Another staggering blow sent him down to his knees, and before he could recover he felt the pavement come up and smash him in the face.

Holloway House Originals by Donald Goines

DOPEFIEND
WHORESON
BLACK GANGSTER
STREET PLAYERS
WHITE MAN'S JUSTICE,
  BLACK MAN'S GRIEF
BLACK GIRL LOST
CRIME PARTNERS
CRY REVENGE
DADDY COOL
DEATH LIST
ELDORADO RED
INNER CITY HOODLUM
KENYATTA'S ESCAPE
KENYATTA'S LAST HIT
NEVER DIE ALONE
SWAMP MAN

Special Preview of *Daddy Cool*—page 161

CRIME PARTNERS

Donald Goines

An Original Holloway House Edition
HOLLOWAY HOUSE PUBLISHING COMPANY
LOS ANGELES, CALIFORNIA

CRIME PARTNERS

An Original Holloway House Edition

This Edition Reprinted 2005

Printed in the United States of America

CRIME PARTNERS
ISBN 0-87067-881-7

WWW.HOLLOWAYHOUSEBOOKS.COM
OR
WWW.HHBOOKSTORE.COM

Dedicated to Shirley Sailor

CRIME PARTNERS

Joe Green, better known to his friends and acquaintances as "Jo-Jo," poured the rest of the heroin out of a small piece of tinfoil into the Wild Irish Rose wine bottle top that had been converted into what drug users call a "cooker."

His common-law wife, Tina, watched him closely. "Damn, Jo-Jo, I sure hate the thought of that being the last dope in the house. The last time your slow-ass connect said he would be here in an hour, it was the next day before the motherfucker showed up!"

Shrugging his thin shoulders philosophically, Jo-Jo didn't even glance up at his woman as he replied. "That's one of the few bad points you run into when

9

your connection doesn't use. They don't understand that a drug addict has to have that shit at certain times. It ain't like a drunk; when Joe Chink says it's time to fix, it's time to fix, with no shit about it."

"Jo-Jo, you don't think the bastard will do us like he did last time, do you?" she asked, her voice changing to a whining, pleading note.

"Goddamn it," Jo-Jo yelled as he patted his pockets, "I ain't got no motherfuckin' matches." He glanced around wildly, his eyes searching in vain for a book of matches on one of the trash-covered end tables.

The house they lived in was a four-room flat. You could enter by either door and stare all the way through the house. The back door led right into the kitchen, which went straight into the dining room, or bedroom, whichever you wanted to call it. The bed came out of the wall, Murphy bed style, and could be put up into the wall after use but never was in this particular house. After the dining room came the front room. Here there had been some sort of effort to gain a partial amount of privacy with a long, filthy bedspread that had been tacked up and stretched across the rooms, separating them. Actually, there were two different bedspreads, each nailed to the ceiling. When a person went between the rooms he parted them in the middle and stepped through, using them the same way you would a sliding door.

"Here, honey," Tina said, holding out a book of matches she had extracted from her purse.

As Jo-Jo leaned over to get the matches his eyes fell on the roll of money in her purse. "Damn, but that seems like a lot of money," he stated, nodding at her open purse.

"Yeah, I know what you mean. It's all those one-dollar bills we took in. Shit, Jo-Jo, we musta taken in over two hundred dollars in singles alone." She smiled suddenly and the smile made the light-complexioned woman look much younger than her twenty-five years. When she smiled the hard lines around her mouth disappeared. Tall, thin, and gaunt to the extent that she appeared to be undernourished, she still retained a small amount of attractiveness.

On the other hand, when Jo-Jo opened his mouth it took something from him. His teeth were rotten, typical of the person who has used hard narcotics for ten years or better. It was catching up with him. He was as slim as his woman.

"Naw, baby, I don't think we'll have the delay we had the last time. Remember on the last cop we were short on the man's money, so I think he did it more or less to teach us a lesson." As he talked, Jo-Jo tore four matches from the book and struck them. He held the burning matches under the cooker until the matches almost burned his fingers. Then he shook the matches out before casually dropping them on the floor.

"Shit! If you had to do the cleaning up, Jo-Jo, you wouldn't be so quick to throw everything you finish with on the damn floor!"

Jo-Jo laughed sharply as he set the hot cooker down on the edge of the coffee table in front of him. His reddish brown eyes surveyed the cluttered floor. There was such an accumulation of trash that it appeared as if no one had bothered to sweep up in over a month. The short brown-skinned man grinned up at his woman. "It don't look as if you been killin' yourself cleaning up."

"Shit!" she snorted again. "If it wasn't for them nasty-ass friends of yours, the place would be clean."

"I'll sweep up for you, Momma," a young voice called out from the dining room-bedroom.

Before either of the grownups could say no, the six-year-old child appeared, pulling a broom along that was taller than she was. Little Tina was a smaller model of her mother, light-complexioned, with dimples in each cheek. She smiled brightly at her mother and stepfather as she tried to make herself helpful.

The appearance of the child didn't stop Jo-Jo in his preparation of the drugs. He removed a stocking from a small brown paper bag, then an eyedropper that had two needles stuck in the bulb part of the dropper. Jo-Jo removed both the needles, then inserted one of them on the end of the dropper.

"Leave me enough to draw up, Jo-Jo," Tina begged before he had even drawn up a drop.

He smiled up at her encouragingly, "Don't worry, honey, don't I always look out for my baby?"

"You can get right funky, Jo-Jo, when the last of the junk is in sight. You're real cool when there's a lot of the jive, but you get doggish as a motherfucker when it ain't but a little bit left."

Unknown to the couple, little Tina had moved closer to the table, swinging the broom back and forth vigorously.

Tina opened up the paper bag and removed another dropper from it. "Is that other spike any good?" she asked anxiously.

"How the fuck would I know?" he cursed sharply as he attempted to open up the needle on his dropper. "This motherfucker of mine is stopped up!"

"No wonder," Tina said as she attempted to draw

up some water from the dirty glass that Jo-Jo was using.

"Your glass has got so much filth in it, it's a wonder you ain't ruined the dope in the cooker." She glanced over his shoulder at the cooker. "You used that water in the glass, didn't you?"

Jo-Jo shrugged. "It don't make no difference, once I put the fire under it. It killed any germs that might have been in the motherfuckin' water."

"Yeah," she answered worriedly, "you may have killed the so-called germs, but what about all that trash we got to draw up?"

In exasperation Jo-Jo cursed, "I don't know what the fuck you want me to do about it. It's done, ain't nothing else I can do. If you're really that motherfuckin' worried over it, Tina, take your ass out to the kitchen and get some more clean water."

"Shit!" she exclaimed, using her stock phrase. "By the time I got back, you'd be done drawin' up all the dope and shot it."

"Goddamn, woman, you don't trust nobody, do you?"

"Daddy, I'll go get you some more water," Little Tina said as she rushed over to the table in an attempt to be helpful. The tall broom she carried was too much for her to control completely. As she neared the table, dragging the broom, the handle swung down in an arc.

Too late, Jo-Jo threw his hand up as if to ward off a blow. The handle came down and struck the cooker, sending it spinning off the end of the table. The drug in the bottom of it spilled out as the top fell off the end of the table onto the dirty throw rug. Instantly the rug absorbed the drug so that it was impossible for the two addicts to save any of it.

Tina dropped down on her knees beside the table. She picked up the overturned cooker. "It wasn't any cotton in the cooker," she stated in a hurt voice. She turned it around and around, as if she couldn't believe it had happened. Suddenly she started to paw at the rug, rubbing it as she searched for some of the liquid that had escaped.

"Not a fuckin' drop left!" she managed to say. "The goddamn rug was like a fuckin' sponge!"

The little girl backed away from the table. Her mouth was open as she pleaded, "I didn't mean it, I'm sorry." Tears ran down both her cheeks.

Instantly Jo-Jo exploded as the sound of her voice brought him out of his trance. He snatched the broom from the child's hand and began beating her about the head with it. With one vicious blow, he broke the broom in half across the child's head.

The little girl attempted to cover up, but it didn't do any good. Jo-Jo snatched her hands down from in front of her face and began to beat her in the face with his fists. He rained blow after blow on the child's exposed face until blood ran from her nose and mouth. When Little Tina fell down at his feet, Jo-Jo drew his foot back and began to kick her viciously in the side.

"You little bitch," he screamed in rage. "God damn you, I done told you to stay the fuck out of the way when I'm makin' up." He grew more angry as he cursed and, instead of the sight of the bleeding child at his feet drawing pity, it only aroused his anger.

Suddenly he reached down and snatched the child to her feet. Her feeble cry of pain only enraged him. "You bitch," he swore over and over, "I'm going to fix your little meddling ass once and for all!"

In pure terror, the girl managed to break away. She

ran back towards the bedroom and attempted to hide under the bed.

Jo-Jo followed closely behind her. He drew his heavy leather belt from off his pants and, grabbing the child's leg, he pulled her from under the bed.

Her screams rang out clear and loud as the belt began to fall, slowly at first and then faster. She squirmed and tried to crawl away from the pain that exploded all over her body. Sometimes the fire would explode on her back, then around her tender legs, but what hurt her the most was when it wrapped around her and the metal part of the belt would dig into her stomach and hips.

"Jo-Jo, Jo-Jo, what you trying to do?" Tina screamed, holding the dividing curtains apart. "If you kill that child, it ain't goin' bring the dope back."

It took a moment for her words to penetrate the blind rage that engulfed him. For a few seconds he couldn't see or think right, but as his senses returned and he saw the bloody child lying on the floor, his anger fled and fear shot through him. Why was she lying so still?

"Tina, Little Tina, get your ass up from there and go in the toilet and wash up," he ordered harshly. He waited impatiently for the child to jump up and obey his order. "Get up," he screamed, his voice breaking slightly. He took his foot and kicked her. "I said get up."

"Don't kick my child," the mother yelled as she came closer. "I done warned you about whipping her so hard, Jo-Jo. If we have to take her to the hospital, I ain't takin' no blame for all those marks on her."

"We ain't going to no hospital," Jo-Jo stated coldly. "All this bitch has got to do is get up and go in the bathroom and wash up. Get up, Tina, I ain't mad no more. I'll get some more stuff later on, don't worry about it," he yelled down at her before kneeling beside her. He put his arms under the frail child's neck and legs, lifted her slowly, and then placed her gently on the bed. He didn't know that it was too late for gentleness now.

"She looks like she's turning blue," Tina screamed out. She frantically clutched at the child. "What's wrong with her? Why is she laying so still? Tina, Tina, wake up girl!"

The mother's fear quickly transferred to the waiting man. Jo-Jo could feel the knot of fear growing in the pit of his stomach. The child couldn't be dead; that he was sure of. He hadn't hit her hard enough for that. No way, he told himself in an attempt to quiet his jumping nerves.

"Oh, Jo-Jo, you got to do something. Man, what's wrong with my little girl? Please, Jo-Jo, do something for her."

If there had been anything he could have done, Jo-Jo would have done it. But he didn't know what to do. All he could do was stare down at the unconscious form and somewhere in the back of his mind he realized what he was too frightened to face. The child was dead. He knew it yet wouldn't face up to the fact.

Little Tina had received her last beating. There would be no more sleepless nights for the child because she was too hungry to sleep. No more lying awake, hoping her mother would come out of her nod long enough to get up and cook something. There would be no more fears of uncontrolled beatings, beatings that came for nothing. Yes, Little Tina was beyond that—beyond a mother's love that sometimes seemed more like hate.

2

The two men sat in the car in front of the shabby frame house. The outside paint job on the house was a battleship gray that looked as if it had seen one battle too many. In many places the paint was peeling, while in others the boards were coming loose.

"Jackie, do you really think this nigger has got some money?" the man on the passenger side of the car asked.

"He's got to have some kind of cash, Billy," the tall, hawk-faced man driving stated clearly. "Just use common sense, Billy Good," he continued, using the man's full name. It was a habit he had adopted from prison, where most men were called by their last names

17

The two men had met in prison ten years ago, and since then they had become rap-partners, having been busted before on an armed robbery charge. Each man had gotten five years out of it, but that had only tightened up the relationship between them. Now, they felt as if they could completely trust each other, each knowing exactly how the other would react during a sudden interruption on one of their many robberies.

"I don't know," Billy began quietly, "I ain't never liked takin' off these small jobs, Jackie. Before we go in the joint we're already up on the fact that we ain't goin' score for no more than a couple of hundred. I mean, it would be different if we were dope addicts or something, but don't either one of us have to have the stuff. Yeah, we'll snort a bit every now and then but that's it. So why should we be frontin' ourselves off for a petty stickup?"

"Goddamn, Billy Good, we went through this shit earlier. You and me both agreed that this would be a safe hit. They ain't goin' call no law in after we leave, plus this punk Jo-Jo ain't nothing but pussy. So it's like takin' candy from a baby. We just walk in and take it, that's all there is to it."

Billy reached over and pushed the cigarette lighter in. "I know, Jackie. Maybe that's what the problem is. I keep rememberin' that cute little kid they got, you know? The last time we were here, she went out of her way to fix me up a glass of cold water. I know it's a small thing, but the kid reminds me of my little girl in New York." Billy removed the lighter and lit his smoke before continuing. "Yeah, I know, a glass of water ain't about nothing, but Jackie, I know the kid's folks ain't got a fuckin' thing, and if we take the little bit they got, it's goin' be just that less that the kid gets."

"That's bullshit, man," Jackie stated harshly. "Dig man, all you got to do is think, Billy. Remember how damn raggedy the child's dress was. Okay, then, it goes to show that the mother ain't even using the fuckin' welfare check they probably get every month for the child. So what we take ain't depriving the child of nothing. What's goin' happen is that they ain't goin' be able to shoot up as much dope this month as they did last month, that's all."

"Ummm-hum, I guess you're just about right," Billy said as he finally made up his mind. "If they were spending any kind of money on that kid it would be food, and as puny as she is I know she's under-fed."

"That's right," Jackie answered quickly. "If they ain't worried about feedin' the kid, you know damn well they ain't worried about what kind of clothes she wears."

Billy laughed suddenly as he opened his car door. "We make a hell of a set of stickup men, Jackie, don't we? Here we are, soft as grapes, worried about some kid."

Jackie saw the humor in it himself. He joined his partner in laughing. He had seen Billy shoot down a woman once without batting an eye, and yet here was the same man worried about taking the food out of a child's mouth. It was a strange world, he reflected, and stranger still were the men and women who lived in it.

As the two men started up the sidewalk it was apparent why the detectives in the holdup department downtown had tagged the crime partners as "Mutt and Jeff." Jackie stood six foot four in his socks, while Billy was only five foot six. But what he didn't have

in height, Billy made up for in width. He was built
like a stocky breeding bull. At first glance he appeared
not to have a neck. Billy was naturally a husky person, but lifting weights in prison had added to his
frame. The huge muscles under his clothes seemed to
roll around as he walked.

Jackie was just the opposite. He was lean to the
point of being almost gaunt. He had the appearance
of a drug addict, even though he was not one yet. But
his love of snorting heroin was leading him down the
path of drug addiction. In time, if he continued to use
drugs at the rate he was doing, he would become an
addict.

When they reached the front door both men hesitated before knocking. Each man checked the pistol
in his waist, making sure the gun didn't protrude.

"Well, baby boy, this is it," Jackie stated calmly as
he raised his fist and knocked. When there was no
sound from inside he knocked louder.

The sudden commotion at the front door startled
the two frightened people inside. Tina jumped as
though she was being shot at. Suddenly a thought
flashed through her mind, and before Jo-Jo could say
anything she fled to the door and jerked it open.

The two men outside the door jumped back, surprised. For a second they thought they had been unlucky
enough to walk up on a bust, but at second glance, they
could see the wild-eyed Tina standing there.

"Please, please, come in. I want you to help me
wake up my baby. She fell and hit her head," Tina
stated as she held the door wide open.

Billy was the first one through the door. For some
reason, the mention of the child put a cold finger of
fear around his heart. As he walked through the front

room, he stepped over the broken broom and noticed the blood spots on the floor.

As soon as he entered the bedroom a feeling of horror washed over him. Nobody had bothered to wash up the child. Her young body was covered with marks from her ordeal. Blood was all over her face and neck, but what really shook Billy was the expression of terror on the child's face. The thought flashed through his mind instantly that this child was beaten to death. Even before he reached the edge of the bed and felt her thin hand he knew she was dead.

When Jackie reached the bed he glanced over at his partner and was surprised to see Billy standing there crying. Tears ran freely down the husky man's cheeks as he held the child's hand helplessly.

"She's dead," Billy stated as if he couldn't believe it. "The kid's dead, Jack!"

Jackie had seen death before, but this was the first time he had ever seen a person who had been beaten to death. "Yeah, she's gone, Billy," Jackie stated, then added, "but she sure in the fuck didn't die from falling and hittin' her head on somethin', man."

"Yes, she did," Jo-Jo answered quickly. "She was running and fell up against the edge of the bed there and cracked her head."

The lie was obvious. There was no reason for the two men to even begin to believe it, but Billy still glanced over to where Jo-Jo said the child had fallen. Instead of seeing what Jo-Jo had wanted him to see, he saw the large leather belt.

"That's what the motherfucker used to beat the child with," Billy said. He pointed the belt out with his finger.

"Yeah," Jackie replied. "He used that and the bro-

ken broom in the next room." When his words didn't
seem to reach Billy, Jackie whirled on his heel and
went back into the front room and picked up the broken broom. He carried it in front of him as if it was
a snake, tossing it at the feet of Billy. "That's one of
the things the motherfucker used. No telling what else
he beat her with."

"Shit!" Tina yelled. "I thought you guys would help
my child, not stand up there and play police. She
needs help!"

As Billy stared at the broken broom the transfor-
mation came over him slowly. The tears on his cheeks
dried up, and his features became rock hard. His pale,
grayish eyes began to glitter dangerously.

"If it's money you want, I got some money," Tina
screamed at the men as she snatched open her purse
and grabbed at the money there. "Here, I'll pay you,
just help me get my daughter to the hospital, that's
all. The doctors can do something for her." Had the
men known more about insanity, they would have
realized that the shock of her child dying had been
too much for the mother. Her mind wouldn't accept
the fact that the child was dead.

"Put that goddamn money up," Jo-Jo ordered harshly.
"If they'll take us to the hospital, I'll pay them for it."

Before Jo-Jo's outstretched hand could reach the
money in Tina's hand, Billy had struck. He whirled
around and swung a left hook to Jo-Jo's midsection. The
punch folded Jo-Jo up, but Billy didn't stop there. He
raised his knee and kicked the man in the face. As Jo-
Jo fell back, Billy followed him, raining punches into
the man's face until Jo-Jo was almost out on his feet.

While this was going on, Jackie didn't waste any
time. He took the pocketbook from the woman and

shook the contents out on the bed. He slowly picked the money up and stuffed it into his pockets while he watched his partner beat Jo-Jo damn near to death.

Suddenly Billy stopped punching the bloody man in front of him. He reached inside his suitcoat, removed his pistol, and slowly raised the gun up until it was pointed right at Jo-Jo's face.

"Man," Jo-Jo managed to say, "what gives with you guys? Take the money, if you want it that bad, but don't hurt us, man. Goddamn, you done hurt me enough already for nothing."

"For nuthin'," Billy mumbled. Then he raised the gun up again and pulled the trigger. The shot tore half of Jo-Jo's face off. Billy pulled the trigger again, blowing the left eye out of the mutilated face. The sound of the gunshots hadn't died down before Tina was rushing over and throwing herself down beside her man.

"Oh God," she screamed loudly, "you done went and killed my man." She raised her finger and pointed at Billy. "I won't forget you, you bastard you," she screamed over and over.

Without a trace of emotion, Billy raised the pistol and shot her in the head. As she fell over beside the dead man, he leaned down and shot her again.

Jackie glanced at the front door nervously, "Okay, baby, it's over with. Let's get the fuck out of here." Without waiting to see if his words had reached home, Jackie started towards the door. He didn't bother to glance back.

When they got to the front door, Jackie glanced up and down the street to see if the gunshots had drawn any attention. But the street was empty, and the men slipped out of the quiet house.

3

Parked outside the dirty frame house were enough police cars to supply a small city with a complete police force—from unmarked cars to the quite visible black-and-white squad cars. The street was full of them, parked on both sides. To the passer-by it looked like a riot or something else as dangerous was about to happen. Police were everywhere asking questions of the people who gathered curiously in front of the small house. As each minute passed, more people arrived. It was as if someone was passing out free meal tickets or passes to the next World Series.

Detective Benson stepped out on the sidewalk and took in a deep breath. It was as though it was the first

time he had been able to breathe fresh air since arriving and entering the house. He glanced back over his
shoulder to see if his partner was coming. While he
waited, two stretcher-bearing hospital attendants came
out of the house carrying a sheet-covered corpse. The
crowd of people milling around in front of the house
got what they had come for. They fell silent as they
watched the men carry the body and place it in the
waiting ambulance. They had waited patiently to see
death, to smell it, and then thank their lucky stars that
it wasn't them on the stretcher.

Benson stared out at the sea of black faces watching him. They were curious about him, another black
man. Yet this one was on the other side of the line.
There he stood, behind the police line where only the
so-called "important people" should be. Benson
removed a cigarette and lit it slowly.

One person in the crowd stared hard at the features
of the black policeman. He took in the short natural
hair style with its accumulation of stray gray hair scat-
tered about. The next thing the watcher noticed was
the chilling black eyes that didn't seem to be searching for anything in particular but from strict custom
were watching the crowd as if it was an enemy. The
large nose gave credence to the rumor that there was
Indian blood in the man. His lips were the lips of a
black man, covered with a heavy black mustache. And
when he smiled, which was seldom, he revealed a
large gap between his teeth that had been with him
since a childhood accident. His shoulders were wide,
tapering off to a narrow waistline, yet at sight of the
man a person would think of strength. It wasn't
because of his size, because he only stood six foot
one, but because of the way he carried himself. He

gave the impression of a coiled snake about to strike. From the burning intensity inside of him, he radiated strength and danger.

Once again Benson glanced over his shoulder to see what could be holding up his partner. He turned on his heel and started back towards the house. On the spur of the moment his feet obeyed a flashing thought and he went around the side of the house. He examined the ground as he walked, looking for anything that might turn out to be a lead. At the rear of the house, he stepped over an overturned garbage can and glanced in the window. There was so much dirt on the window sill that he knew at once that nobody had used this particular window in some time.

"By God, hold it, nigger; right there." The harsh southern voice filled Benson with a cold, murderous rage. Before he turned around and faced the man with the harsh voice, Benson fought to control his temper. He knew that, if he turned around at once, he would end up by taking the loud-mouthed officer apart.

"Put your hands up on that fuckin' wall," the officer ordered loudly. "What's wrong, boy? You hard of hearing or something, nigger?" the policeman continued as Benson refused to follow his demand.

No matter what you did, or what you became, the thought flashed through Benson's mind, you'd always be a nigger to some of these hillbilly bastards. The word didn't disturb him but the tone of voice the speaker used did. Even though he hadn't done anything, this bastard was ready to kill him. Benson didn't fool himself by taking any chances, because he knew the officer standing behind him would do just that if he was given any kind of reason. That white bastard would take his life for no other reason except for the fact that Benson was black.

"Nigger, I ain't goin' waste my time tellin' you again to raise your arms and stretch out against that wall," the policeman stated coldly.

For the first time since the officer had come up behind him, Benson started to speak. "Listen, mack," he began, "I'm a detective with the first precinct. My badge is inside my coat pocket along with my gun, so don't get carried away." He almost smiled in the dark, glad that he had been able to control his voice. The boiling, raging anger inside of him was mounting to an unbearable pitch, his anger and frustration like a deep river that was slowly rising. He knew he had to prevent it at all costs. He could not gratify his desire by taking it out on the ignorant bastard behind him.

The sudden feel of cold blue steel being pressed against his back blew his mind. In another second he would have exploded into action, but the sound of a new voice arrested his action.

"Well, what have we got here?" At the sound of the voice, Benson turned around and faced the two officers. The first policeman, standing directly behind him, started to get red in the face.

"By God, I thought I told you to put your fuckin' hands up against the wall," he snarled angrily.

Benson didn't bother to glance at the new arrival. "I don't know what they teach you new rookies, you dumb sonofabitch, but I've told you once that I'm an officer—a fuckin' detective at that!" He glared at the man, his anger obvious to both of the uniformed men. "Now, boy," and he dragged the word out, "I'm going to take your badge number and see to it that your fuckin' ass is lit up for this shit you tried to pull on me back here."

The red-faced officer was out of his depth. There was no doubt in his mind now that the black man in front of him was what he said he was. He wished silently that he had pulled the trigger when he had the opportunity. Then it would have been just an accident. But now, he didn't know where he stood. He glanced over at the other officer. It was his partner, true enough, but he didn't know how far his partner would go. He glanced down at the pistol still in his hand. All he'd have to do would be to pull the trigger.

As if he had read the policeman's mind, Benson pushed the gun away. "I don't like havin' guns pointed at me." He pulled out his wallet and flipped open the leather, revealing his badge. "You," he pointed out the new arrival, "I want this man written up." With a nod of his head, he ordered the two men towards the front of the house. "What's your name?" Benson asked of the second policeman.

"Kelly, sir," the young, boyish-looking officer replied quickly. Kelly silently thanked his lucky stars that he hadn't been in the rear with his partner. He didn't have to be there to realize what had happened. He had warned Jim, his partner, that his race hatred would get him in trouble. Nowadays you couldn't tell what a black man might be, so you didn't treat them all as if they were dirt. But he couldn't get it through Jim's thick head, so he'd have to learn the hard way that those days of abusing every black person you came in contact with were over.

As they approached the front of the house, a tall blond-haired detective came towards them. "God damn it, there you are. I wondered where in the fuck you had gone."

Benson didn't smile at his partner's approach. The

frown on his face was one that Ryan was well famil-
iar with. "Both of you guys wait right here," Benson
ordered sharply.

"Like hell we will," the officer called Jim stated
loudly. "I don't know when we started taking orders
from you."

Before Benson could reply, Ryan took it up. "I don't
know what the problem is here, son, but whenever a
detective gives an order it's generally obeyed by an
officer."

"I haven't said anything," Kelly stated, trying to
make sure he wasn't caught up in whatever was about
to jump off.

Benson pulled Ryan to the side and explained
everything, even adding the thought that he believed
the officer would have shot him if it hadn't been for
the arrival of his partner. As Benson talked, Ryan's
eyes grew hard until they were mere pinpoints. He
had worked with this black man for over two years
now, and in that time they had both saved each other's lives on more than one occasion

As soon as Benson finished talking, Ryan whirled
around on the two policemen. "He told you once; now
I'm giving my order. I want both of you to wait right
here until I speak with the captain." Ryan removed
his pad from his pocket and wrote both the men's
badge numbers down. In a few minutes he was back,
walking alone across the lawn.

At the sight of Ryan reappearing by himself Jim
felt a little better. They couldn't do too much to him
for making a small mistake. How the hell could he
tell that the nigger was an officer? One black face was
like another as far as he was concerned.

"You know," Jim began, trying to appear friendly

to Benson, "this was a mistake any man could make. I mean, if I had been back there out of uniform you would have probably made the same mistake," he stated, then laughed loudly.

Ryan still had that cold look about him as he walked up. "You boys can go about your business now. The captain said he'd like to see both of you downtown in his office tomorrow morning at ten o'clock. Then we can get to the bottom of this mess."

"Gee whiz," Kelly said over and over, "I don't know anything about this crap. All I did was walk into the rear of the house to find my partner, that's all."

"You did more than you realize," Benson stated shortly. "If you hadn't appeared when you did, I'm sure your partner here would have found reason to shoot me."

"Aw, come on now, buddy. It wasn't that bad, and you know it. Why, it was only a mistake. I can't understand why you don't just let the matter drop. After all, we're both on the same side, right?"

"Wrong. Your kind of man should never be allowed to wear a uniform, and I'm going to do everything in my power to see if I can't get you out of that uniform."

"Okay, you guys, we'll see you downtown tomorrow. Come on, Ed," Ryan said, using Benson's first name, "let's get on our way. We've got some murders to solve!"

Edward Benson slowly walked with his partner out to their car, which was parked at the curb. The two uniformed officers followed them closely.

"Man, oh man, you sure put your fuckin' foot in it that time, didn't you, Jim?" Kelly stated matter-offactly. "Of all the spades you had to run into, it would have to be that guy there."

"Okay, okay," Jim replied, "but I don't see why it has to be so bad. That fuckin' guy ain't that much, is he?"

Kelly just shook his head as he watched the two men get in the unmarked car. How he wished that he was the one getting into an unmarked car and wearing plain clothes. Well, if he kept his nose clean he would reach that goal one day.

"I don't know what to say, Jim. We can only wait until tomorrow and see what kind of charges they draw up against you."

"By God," Jim drawled angrily, "I don't see how they can take a fuckin' nigger's word over mine. If they do, I'm damn sure workin' on the wrong job."

Kelly only shrugged his shoulders. You dumb hillbilly bastard, he said under his breath. Maybe it would work out for the best. After all, Kelly reasoned, he just might come up with a real intelligent partner—someone he'd have something in common with.

Neither detective spoke as Ryan pulled away from the curb. They had worked together so long that both men knew when the other was in a compatible mood. Ryan realized that Ed had been hurt tonight, even though he would never admit it. A fellow officer had disrespected him to a point where he was moody and dangerous.

Brooding wouldn't solve it, so Ryan decided to try to take Benson's mind off his problem. "Hey, man, I'm goin' to need you on this case. We got three brutal murders on our hands, so come off it. You ain't no goddamn kid, you know."

When Benson didn't answer, Ryan continued. "The

way I got it figured, whoever the bastards were that did this shit, they tortured the kid to force information out of the parents."

"I don't know, Ryan; that's pure speculation there. I don't like it for some reason. It's too pat. Even when you theorize it like that, it jumps into a set pattern. The child was beaten, that's for sure. But tortured, well that's a different matter altogether." Benson slowly rubbed his nose. "I examined the body closely, Ryan, and there was something there that I either overlooked or just don't have the knowledge to put it together. I want a look at the coroner's report first thing in the morning."

"I think," Ryan began, "you're making a mountain out of a fuckin' molehill. Both the parents were drug addicts, so we got the reason for torture, if torture was indeed used. Next, if we find out these people were dealing, the damn case will bust itself open. Drugs, that's the only answer. Drugs are the reason this brutal crime was committed, and I'll bet my check against a full bucket of shit!"

Benson glanced over at his partner. "This case kind of hits you below the belt, huh, John?

Ryan shrugged, then answered, "You know I got this thing about kids, Ed. I can't help myself. I love 'em. I don't care if they're brown, blue, green, or white. I love kids period."

Benson knew what his partner said was true. Sometimes after work, you could find Ryan in the nearest gym, teaching young boys how to play basketball. It didn't make any difference what color the kid was. Ryan taught them all.

"You know, Ryan, it's guys like you that makes me want to put a fuck on the whole white race. You good behavior guys!" Benson laughed briefly.

"Yeah, I just know you do," Ryan answer quickly. "The only thing in the white race you want to fuck is everything in a skirt." They laughed together. The tension had been broken.

Ryan drove over to an all-night drive-in restaurant, and the two men sat in the car and ordered dinner. They remained quiet until after their food had come and gone.

"This is going to be kind of a hard one to bust open, Ed. We haven't found one good witness yet."

"I don't know about that, Ryan. If it's like you say, and I don't have any reason to doubt it, maybe the narcotics department can come up with some kind of help. Drug addicts aren't the most closed-mouthed people in the world. So suppose we put out the word. Just maybe somebody will talk. A killin' like this can't remain quiet. Somebody somewhere knows something, and if we push in the right direction, something will have to give."

Ryan waited until after he started up the car and pulled out into the late-night traffic. "I pray to God that you're right about that, Ed," he stated. "I want this one. I want it bad. I want those killers, and I want them as soon as possible."

4

It was past two o'clock in the afternoon when Billy and Jackie started to get up. Jackie remained stretched out in the bed even after he heard Billy up and around in the next bedroom. The picture of the killings that had occurred the past evening was still in Jackie's mind. He wondered if Billy was ever bothered by the images of the people they had killed. It was something Jackie couldn't get out of his system. That's why he believed he'd never be a real killer. Not the kind of cold-blooded killer you saw in the movies or on television.

"Why don't you run down to the drug store and get the morning paper, Billy? Maybe they got something in it about us."

In a second Billy's head appeared in Jackie's doorway. "There you go again, man, lookin' for them headlines."

Billy sat on the edge of his partner's bed. "Look, baby, if you want to see yourself or read about yourself in the paper, we got to take off the big one. These little petty capers like last night, they won't even make the back paper, let alone the front page."

For a brief minute Jackie remained silent, staring up from the bed at his partner. "Is that all last night was to you, Billy? Just another caper? Is that all, man?"

Billy stared at him strangely. "What's this shit, man? I don't dig where you're coming from. Of course that's all it was, a caper. If you're thinkin' about that couple, think about that kid and what them funky motherfuckers did to her. Think about that, Jackie! About the expression on her face when she died. Then if you have any pity left, tell me about it."

"I read you loud and clear, Billy. That's all I needed to get my thinking cap on right, too. But I'd still like to see if there was anything in the papers about us."

Billy grinned at his friend. "I know, nigger. By the time you got out of the bed they'd be done sold out of papers. Then we'd have to wait for the evening paper to come out. Okay, my man, I'll be your flunky this time, but I don't promise you the same kind of action this time tomorrow."

The men laughed together, then Billy got up and went out to get the paper. While he was gone, Jackie climbed out of the bed and took a quick shower. He wished he had a blow. One quick snort would really put his think cap on right. The more he thought about it, the more he wanted some dope.

Jackie paced up and down the apartment, wearing

nothing but a huge white towel. Suddenly he made up his mind. Picking up the phone, he dialed the number of an apartment two floors above the one he lived in. He knew the woman upstairs had some drugs. That wasn't the problem. The problem was getting her to bring it downstairs. As a last resort, he reasoned, he could always slip on something and run up the stairs and get it himself.

"Hello, Lucy. Hi, baby. This is Jackie. You know, Jackie, the tall guy who stays downstairs under you, baby. Yeah, I thought you'd realize who it was. Look, honey, would you do me a favor? No, baby, let me finish, I don't want any credit. Naw, nothing like that. When I say favor, I just mean I'd like to ask if you would send me a twenty-five-dollar package down here. I'm kind of tied up right now or I'd run up myself and get it."

He held the phone closely as he listened, then cut her off. "Listen, woman. I don't play games. Your money is here. I'm just asking you to do me a favor and send it down. I don't care who brings it, you or the man in the moon. I just don't give a fuck. All I want is the stuff. Hey, wait a minute, momma, I ain't no petty nigger. Naw, baby, if I was goin' rip off something, it would be a hell of a lot bigger than a twenty-five-dollar bag."

Again he waited patiently until she stopped talking, then he inquired sharply, "Listen, baby, if I wasn't tied up, I'd have run upstairs and got it. By now, I could have been upstairs and back. If you ain't goin' do it, just say so. All this bullshit you're taking me through ain't worth it. I asked you to do me a favor. Whether or not you do it is up to you. Are you going to send it or not?"

For an instant Jackie started to slam the receiver down on the woman, then he curbed his temper. "Listen, girl, I just got out of the shower and I ain't got no clothes on. If you're going to send it, send it right now. If it ain't here by the time I get dressed, I'll figure it ain't coming." With that said, he slammed the phone down and stalked back to his closet. He rummaged through the few clothes hanging up inside. There wasn't much to choose from, because Jackie wasn't what you would call a dresser. In fact, he rarely went out of his way to buy clothes. Only when Billy went shopping and dragged him along would he pick out something. He had two suits and four pairs of stray pants, plus a variety of shirts. And the few clothes were in various conditions, with some dirty while others were still in cleaners' bags.

Without really caring what he wore, Jackie removed a dark blue pair of pants from the closet and put them on quickly. He was in the process of picking out a clean shirt when the doorbell rang. Without bothering to put the shirt on, he walked back into the front room and jerked the door open.

The sudden opening of the door took the woman by surprise. Her mouth opened and she gave a frightened little yell before gaining control of herself. She must have really been frightened after all, Jackie reasoned, as he stared down at her. The bitch really thought I was planning on knockin' her off for the fuckin' twenty-five-dollar bag, he thought as he examined her frightened face.

"Come on in for a second, honey," Jackie said softly as he reached out and took her hand. "I just slipped these goddamn pants on and left my bankroll in the bedroom." He almost dragged tbe plump, brown-skinned woman into the living room. "Just relax, Lucy, I ain't goin' be but a minute," he stated, dropping her hand. "Make yourself at home, have a set, relax, take the weight off your feet."

Lucy finally managed to find her voice. "No, I don't have the time. I left the kids by themselves because I knew it wouldn't take but a minute for me to run down here and drop this off." She had to raise her voice because he had disappeared into the bedroom.

In a second Jackie reappeared, carrying the money in his hand. "Thanks, Lucy, I appreciate your bringing the stuff down here, honey. If I hadn't just come out of the shower I wouldn't have put you to so much trouble."

She took the money from his outstretched hand. "It wasn't no trouble, really. You know, Jackie, I ain't got but a few customers, so I sure didn't want to make you angry with me." She stood up to go, then added, "Sometimes, Slim, when you ain't doing nothing, come on up and keep me and the kids company. I'll lay out the blow for you."

As she started to the door, Jackie glanced at the heavy hips swinging back and forth. Not bad, he reasoned. She was in her early thirties, still built fairly well, and hadn't had but three kids. The woman was probably lonely, plus half scared to death. It was dangerous selling drugs, even for a man. A woman dealing for herself was open game. It took a hell of a lot of nerve.

"I might just take you up on that, Lucy," he said quietly as he held the door open for her. She slipped the small package into his hand, smiled brightly up at him, then walked away, swinging her hips even more than before.

"Well, I'll be a motherfucker! I ain't gone over five minutes and this cocksucker done pulled a big-hip broad," Billy roared as he came down the hall.

Jackie cursed under his breath. He had wanted to get into the package before Billy returned. Not that Billy would have wanted any, but he just hadn't wanted Billy to know he had it.

Billy closed the door behind him. "Ain't that the old bitch who deals upstairs?" he inquired as he flopped down in the nearest chair.

"Yeah, Billy. I had her bring me a small blow. You care for a little toot?" Jackie asked as he opened up the tinfoil and dumped the white powder out.

Billy shook his head. "Naw, man, it's way too early in the day for me. That shit would have me puking up and down the street. I couldn't take care of no kind of business whatsoever."

"Actually, Billy Good, I didn't know we had any business to take care of today. In fact, I was under the impression this was going to be our day off. That's why I bought this bag."

"Uh-huh," Billy mumbled while he coldly reflected that it was getting to where any reason was an excuse for Jackie to get a bag. "I ran into Kenyatta's woman while I was at the store. She said the dude was in shape, so we can drop by there and pick up some pieces that we need."

Tearing off a piece of his matchbook cover, Jackie folded it until he had made a small shovel. Then he used it to push the heroin into his nose. He waited until he had snorted over half the pile.

"I wonder how much Kenyatta is going to charge us for some guns this time. I swear, that black bastard jacks the price every time we buy from him,"

Jackie stated, his voice dragging as he spoke. He began to scratch his nuts as he added, "I wish we had another connect somewhere."

"Man, man, man, don't nothin' make you happy? We got one of the coolest gun connects in the fuckin' world, yet you ain't satisfied. You still complain." Billy shrugged his shoulders then continued. "I don't care who we deal with, they ain't goin' be no better than Kenyatta. You can bet your motherfuckin' ass on it, too."

"I don't know why you dig the cat so much, Billy. When we hit on him to loan us two good men so that we could take off that big caper, what did the guy do? He went to nut city on us. That's what the motherfucker did. If he'd been cool we would be rolling in bread right now."

"I don't know about that, Jackie. He might still go along with it. It depends on certain things being right, that's all."

Both men fell silent, and Jackie snorted a small pile of dope before saying, "Well, ain't no sense in us laying around the pad all day. Let's make some kind of move."

"That's okay with me," Billy replied quickly. "Let's go over and check on the guns first. After that, I'm goin' find me some soul food."

Ten minutes later the men came out of the apartment. They climbed into a black Ford that Billy had rented the day before. Billy drove slowly, following the traffic until they reached Clay Street. He parked in front of a store-front building that had an apartment over it. Four young black men were loitering in front of the building, and they watched the two men get out of the car with a casual interest.

"What's happenin', brothers?" Billy said as they

came abreast of the men. The group of brothers nodded in return. "You guys know whether or not
Kenyatta is on the set?" Billy inquired as he stopped
in front of the group.

"Yeah, brother, he's right inside," one of the men said
quietly, then added. "What you guys want with him?"

The question took Billy by surprise, but Jackie
answered for both of them. "Hey, brother, your name
ain't Kenyatta, is it?" Jackie asked the man sharply.
Then he added before the man could reply, "No, I did-
n't think so," and pushed open the door.

The group could only stare at the back of the tall
man as he went through the door last. Billy glanced
back over his shoulder at Jackie, who winked at him,
causing both men to break out laughing.

The inside of the building was furnished cheaply.
There were wooden chairs in the outside waiting
room, along with an old worn desk that had seen better days. On the walls were pictures of Che, Ho Chi
Min, and other men of color who were dedicated lead-
ers in various revolutions.

A young black girl sat behind the desk reading a
novel, and she glanced up at their approach. "Can I
help you?" she inquired in a soft voice.

Billy glanced at her closely. "Yeah, baby, you could
if you'd only be willing." He leaned over the desk
and stared down her open blouse.

The young girl blushed slightly, then looked away.

"We'd like to see Kenyatta, miss," Billy stated
quickly, not wanting to really embarrass the woman.

She almost jumped up from the chair she had been
sitting in. "I'll have to go see if he's in," she stated,
as she walked quickly towards the closed door in the
rear of the building.

"Boy, I wish I had that effect on women," Jackie said quietly, glancing around the room "Man, that old girl couldn't get away from you quick enough. I'd be willing to bet that you scared her so bad she peed on herself."

"Bullshit," Billy replied. "She was just in a hurry to take care of my request, that's all."

"Yeah, I dug it. She was in such a hurry that she didn't even bother to get our names," Jackie answered as the door in the rear opened.

A tall black man came out, dressed in a pair of old Levis that had seen better days. The white T-shirt he wore was spotlessly clean. He was completely bald, and his head had been greased until it had a shine to it. The only hair he possessed was his beard and mustache. The beard was heavy, running around his cheeks until it would have met his sideburns if he had had any. The most remarkable thing about him was the jet black eyes that stared out without blinking, giving him a hawkish look that went well with the long, keen nose he had.

When he spoke his voice was so heavy that it sounded as if he was talking from inside a barrel. "I'll be goddamned," he began, "what have we here?"

"What's happenin', Kenyatta?" Billy said quickly, glancing away from the man. From past experience, Billy knew he couldn't stand to look the man in the eye. It gave him the feeling that Kenyatta was reading his thoughts.

"Why don't you and your partner come in the rear? We can talk better from my office," Kenyatta stated as he turned his back to the men and led the way back the way he had come.

No one spoke until after they entered the well-furnished rear office. The carpet on the floor was a dark brown, which matched the other furnishings in the room. Posters hung on the walls, but there were paintings of black women and men hanging there also. The paintings were well done.

Kenyatta waved his hand toward two comfortable, over-stuffed chairs. "You guys make yourselves at home," he said as he walked around the oval desk and sat down in an expensive chair.

Two young black girls sitting in the office got up to go. "Ken," the taller of the two said, "is there anything we can do for you before we leave?" she asked in a velvet voice.

Kenyatta glanced over at his guests. "Can I have the ladies fix you up something?" he asked. "Maybe a hard drink, or some pop or coffee?"

The tall black woman waited patiently for the men to make up their minds. "I wouldn't mind some tea, if you have any hot," Billy said, leering at the woman.

Jackie shook his head. "Yeah, I'll have the same thing, with plenty sugar."

"You like what you see, Billy?" Kenyatta asked as the two women started out the door. "The tall sister is my lady, but I don't mind someone admiring her." There was a note of pride in his voice as he spoke.

"Yeah, baby, it really makes a person realize what they mean when they say black is beautiful," Billy replied honestly. "I got to give you credit, baby boy, you really have a lady there."

"Beauty is only skin deep, Billy," Kenyatta answered slowly, then added, "but in her case, she is really something else. Besides her good looks she's a lady, inside and out. A black lady."

"Is there any difference?" Jackie asked sharply.

"You can bet your ass on it," Kenyatta answered quickly. "There's nothing under the sun like a black lady, brother."

"Well, from what I just saw, I'd say there ain't many black ladies like the one that just walked out of here," Billy said quickly.

Kenyatta laughed. "Well, like the white man would ask, what brought you brothers over here today? I know you didn't come just to admire my woman, so give me an idea of what it really is."

"Guns!" Billy stated harshly. "We need some more pieces as soon as possible."

Kenyatta got up from behind his desk and walked up and down the room. "You use a lot of guns, man. I mean, you two guys are really good customers. If I were in the gun business, I'd make plenty bread off you two. But," he continued, before either man could say anything, "since I'm not in the gun business, every time I sell you guys guns, you're taking guns away from my men."

Billy waited until the man paced back towards them before saying in a joking manner, "Well, baby, we might even join your organization one day."

Kenyatta stopped his pacing. "No, I couldn't use you brothers, I don't think. I know you got the nerve, but you're just not the type for my thing. My boys have got to be dedicated. You brothers are dedicated, but not to gettin' rid of these white pigs that ride around our neighborhoods acting like white gods."

"Shit!" Jackie cursed loudly, "when it comes to gettin' rid of some white cops, man, I'd gladly go along with it, just for the fun of it. The way I hate Whitey, I pray for the chance to knock off one of the bastards any time I can."

"I wish that were true," Kenyatta stated, staring at the man closely.

"It's true," Billy stated, "and I feel the same way my man does."

As Kenyatta stared from one man to the other, the door opened and the tall sister came in carrying a tray with their drinks on it. The men remained silent until the woman had come and gone, but all the time she was there Kenyatta never took his eyes off of them.

"If what you guys say is true, I'll give you a chance to earn them guns you want," Kenyatta stated quietly. "I'm going out on a small job tonight, to rid the neighborhood of two nigger-haters that work the afternoon shift. If you and your partner will go along on the hit with us, I'll give you both whatever kind of guns you want when we get back."

Billy had to swallow twice before he could speak. "You mean you goin' knock off some white cops tonight?" he asked softly, not realizing how low his voice had dropped.

"I mean some white-ass pigs are going to meet their fuckin' maker tonight, whether or not you two guys go along with the program or not," Kenyatta answered, his voice revealing the anger that he felt towards the white officers he spoke of. "Yeah," he continued, "it's goin' sure as hell be tonight."

"It sounds good to me," Jackie said as he grinned at his partner. "I don't even need the promise of the guns. Just the thought of gettin' rid of some of them motherfuckers is enough for me."

"Well, not me," Billy said quickly. "I got to know if it's planned right and everything. You just don't knock off cops unless you got it down tight."

"How you think all them white cops that've been

gettin' knocked off in this city got hit? If it hadn't been right, somebody would have been busted by now," Kenyatta stated, not bragging but just stating a fact.

"You mean you and your boys are responsible for them hits we been reading about in the papers?" Billy asked.

"Do you know of any other niggers in this city with enough balls to knock off a cop?" Kenyatta slowly asked, watching the two men in front of him closely.

"I thought," Billy began, "that you were only responsible for the hits being made on the dope men in various neighborhoods."

"That too is part of our program," Kenyatta replied, "but not just that. Somebody has to rid the city of these funky white cops, and we are doing that." Again he glanced closely at the two men, then added, "I'm waiting on a list of dope men—big ones—not just neighborhood pushers, and when I get the list, brother, you ain't read nothing in the papers yet compared to what will be in them then."

"A list!" Jackie said. "You mean with the names of white suppliers, the dagos, and other big men?" His voice held the note of disbelief in it that Kenyatta had become accustomed to hearing whenever he mentioned the list to other people.

"That's right, little brother, I got a dago gettin' it together for me. He's chargin' over ten grand just for the list," Kenyatta said truthfully.

"Ten grand!" Billy exploded. "You mean you're going to shell out that kind of dough just for a piece of paper with some names of dope pushers on it?"

"Not just some dope pushers, but the top pushers in the motherfuckin' city. Every motherfuckin' honkie that has his hand in dope. When I get that I'm goin'

cause such a panic in this city for dope that a dope
fiend had better catch the first thing smokin' towards
Chicago or New York, 'cause there won't be any dope
coming in for quite a while."

"That's quite a program you've cut out for yourself, man," Jackie stated. There was a note in his voice
that revealed that he didn't really believe what the
man in front of him was saying. He didn't want to
come out and call Kenyatta a liar, but it was there in
his voice for anyone to hear.

"Yeah, brother, I don't ask you to believe me. Just
have a little patience, and I'll prove it to you. When
it jumps off, I'll have some work for you boys, 'cause
I'll be needin' outside help every now and then."

"Yeah, my man," Jackie began, "you're definitely
giving yourself a big job, brother. And if it's like you
say, you're going to need everybody you can get. Not
only us, but fifty more men just like us."

Kenyatta shook his head. "Don't think I'm a fool,
brother, 'cause I ain't. I've got twenty-five men, plus
fifteen women who are in our organization, and every
one of them is dedicated, so l ain't foolin' myself. My
people are trained, and every one of them has one
thought in their mind. Kill the honkie. That's our rally
cry. Death to Whitey."

As he spoke, his voice rose with the power of his
conviction. Jackie thought to himself that this brother is mad. He's stone crazy; he believes every fuckin'
thing he's saying. There was no doubt in either man's
mind of that. Kenyatta was serious about everything
he said. The thought of him having over forty people
believing in him was crazy in itself. That many people following in his path would give a madman quite
a bit of power.

Kenyatta leaned over the desk, staring at the men in front of him. His eyes were lit up with an unholy glow that burned too brightly. There was madness there, yet the fire that burned there was also the mark of the strong man, a leader, the kind of man the people could follow with complete trust. "It can be done!" he stated, pounding on the desk to get his point across. "It can be done, and it will be done. This city will be rid of dope pushers and race-hatin' cops. You can bet on it."

"I believe you, brother. When you state it like that I can't help but believe you," Billy said truthfully. And at the time he did believe. It was one of Kenyatta's strong points, the ability to make people believe in his dream. Whether he could make it true or not, he could make people believe in him.

As he talked, Jackie was visualizing Kenyatta talking in front of an audience, the gestures the man would use, the way he had of standing with his head thrown back. He would and could impress a lot of people.

Jackie smiled encouragingly. "Man, you got something about you, Kenyatta. I don't know what it is, but you got it, brother."

"Yeah, man," Billy agreed. "The man sure got something about him. Here he done talked us into going on quite a job with him tonight, free of charge. If that ain't the power of persuasion I don't know what is."

"Wait a second, Billy," Jackie said slowly. "I ain't agreed to nothin' yet. I want to hear how we're supposed to go about this hit before I give my okay on it. I ain't just jumpin' up and shootin' no cops without knowin' if it's goin' be a way to get away or not. I don't plan on gettin' busted for killing no police. Not this boy. My mother ain't had no fools that I know of."

Kenyatta studied Jackie icily. "Whether or not you agree, brother, you're in it now. You know too much about it for me to let you walk out of here. It's damn near impossible for you not to go on it, if you know what I mean."

"Naw, man, I don't know what you mean. If you're thinkin' about making us prisoners in this mother-fucker, I don't think I'd dig that," Jackie stated sharply, slowly getting out of his chair.

Kenyatta waved him back down. "Just stop a minute, brother, and think. If you're for real, it shouldn't disturb you that I'm taking no risks. I can't risk my men by allowing you to leave. No way. It just can't be done."

"Shit!" Jackie got up, towering over the man by at least four inches, but Kenyatta didn't back down. "I don't like the idea of being held against my will by anyone, Kenyatta," he said. His face was a mirror of his feelings, filled with anger.

"Just hold on, partner," Billy said quickly, getting to his feet also. "Kenyatta is cool, man, so don't get upset."

"All we goin' do," Kenyatta began, "is stay upstairs until time to leave tonight. I'll run it all down to you when we get upstairs, and I promise you, you'll dig it."

Billy patted his partner on the back. "Be cool, man; everything is going to be all right. Have I ever led you wrong, Jackie? I mean it, man. You're my part-ner, so I'm asking you, buddy, to just have faith in me this time. You know, I don't ask that lightly, Jackie, so just do me the favor and trust in me. Okay?"

Jackie stared at his partner. "When you put it that way, I have to go along with the program, but I don't like it, baby. I don't like it at all."

Kenyatta smiled encouragingly at the men as he came around the desk and patted them on the shoulder. "Don't worry, my man, I trust you. And I know you been fuckin' with some dope, so if I can trust a would-be dope fiend, I believe you should be able to put a little faith in me."

As Jackie scowled angrily, Billy laughed out loud. "He's got us there, Jackie. The man ain't too far wrong. Jackie, you done had a blow, so if he can trust us, we should be able to put a little faith in him."

"Yeah, baby, yeah," Jackie replied as he followed to the door, but he didn't like it one bit. "All I got to say is that the plan had better be a good one."

"It's a good one," Kenyatta answered as he led the way toward a side door that led upstairs. "It's so good you'll fall in love with it!" He laughed loudly as they began the climb up the narrow stairway. At the top, a closed heavy oak door greeted the men, and as they approached the door an eye peeped through a small slit. At sight of Kenyatta, the door began to open, and as the men entered the apartment the sound of female laughter came to them.

"Well, the way them women sound, I might enjoy my short stay up here after all," Billy stated as he glanced around, trying to catch sight of the women.

"I'm quite sure you'll enjoy it," Kenyatta stated, "'cause all we goin' do is have big fun until time to go. Yeah," he repeated, "I really mean big fun."

5

As the evening wore on, Kenyatta made sure none of the people participating in the coming ordeal used too much alcohol. When Billy had a girl fix him another drink, Kenyatta overlooked the fact until Billy tried a few minutes later to get another one. Then, and only then, did Kenyatta speak up.

"Hey, baby, what you goin' do?" he asked jokingly. "I know we're all grown," he said, "but we might need you straight-eyed, if you know what I mean. If something should jump off wrong, man, and you have to foot it, them drinks would cut off your breath. You'd fuck around and find yourself short-winded when you might just need to be long-winded."

Everybody joined in the laughter, including Jackie, who had started to enjoy himself. The young brown-skinned girl sitting on his lap bounced around play-fully. The other men and women smoked reefers and joked among themselves until it was time to go. Kenyatta's woman, Betty Jean, got up from the couch where she had been sitting. Every man's eyes followed her as she made her way across the floor. It wasn't because she walked sexy, but she was so attractive that she drew men the way a fire draws moths. She couldn't help herself, just as they couldn't help but look. The tight black pants she wore didn't help mat-ters any.

When she reentered the room, she was carrying a small suitcase. She glanced over to Kenyatta, who was sitting on the couch. He got up and took the suitcase from her, then walked back to the couch and dumped the contents of the bag on the marble-topped coffee table. The guns were scattered out on the table, mak-ing an assortment of pistols, from thirty-eights down to a small twenty-two automatic.

As the five men in the room came over to the table, Kenyatta let his eyes run over the front-room apart-ment. Idly he wondered if he would make it back to his room that he liked so much. The thick carpet on the floor was the same deep brown as that which had been used downstairs. It came with the deal that fur-nished the office. One large roll of expensive carpet had been stolen from a warehouse across town and found its way to Kenyatta's place. He had had his office downstairs carpeted, as well as the whole upstairs, for less than one hundred dollars.

The rest of the furniture in the apartment matched the carpet and was expensive also. The couch had matching chairs in light tan, while the end tables were all marble-topped. The front room led into the living room, which was large and roomy, yet not so large as to appear spacious. The dining room set was dark brown, with a matching china cabinet. The chairs around the table were all deep-cushioned, again looking expensive. The cost at a store would have been over a thousand dollars, but again it came from across town, from a warehouse, costing Kenyatta less than two hundred dollars.

"Take it easy," Kenyatta said as the men shoved each other in their haste to get the gun of their choice. "It's enough pieces there for everybody. If you don't find what you like, just holler. We'll see to it that you get what you're lookin' for."

"How many can a man take?" a thin boy in his early twenties asked, picking up a small pistol and examining it closely. "I'd like to have this little piece in case I get uptight with the law."

"Shit, Big-Time," a short, light-complexioned man said, "that thing ain't got enough power to knock down a fly!"

"Hey, Red, I ain't lookin' for power with this," Big-Time answered, grinning at the man. Red grinned back, revealing a mouthful of rotten teeth. There was a gap in the front of his mouth, showing where a tooth had been knocked out sometime in the man's past.

Red fumbled with the lock on a German Luger, undecided on whether or not to use it or a thirty-eight that he liked. As he handled each weapon, Jackie reached over and picked up the thirty-eight.

"Hey, man, don't you see me checkin' out that piece?" Red stated sharply, trying to snatch the gun back out of Jackie's hand.

"Be cool, boy, you don't snatch something from a man. If you want it, ask, but don't snatch, you dig?" Jackie checked the man loudly.

As the men glared at each other, Kenyatta waited to see if they would handle it without getting into an argument. The last thing he wanted was to see his men start arguing among themselves.

Red glanced up at the large man. "Goddamn, brother, I ain't got no misunderstanding with you. Hell no, you're too fuckin' big for me to even dream of fightin' with, let alone really fall out with."

Kenyatta grinned. He knew that Red had as much nerve as any man in the room, if push came to shove. He knew that Red could more than handle himself. Every man in his organization had been trained to use judo, the deadly art of death. How to kill with the bare hands was something he taught every man and woman who joined his outfit.

Jackie grinned down at the smaller man. "That's all right, brother," he said and held out the gun. "Here, my man, I just wanted to see how the handle was made. If you decide not to use it though, let me know. I'm kind of fond of thirty-eights."

"What time are we supposed to leave?" Billy asked from where he was sitting, checking out different guns.

"It's just about that time," Kenyatta answered as he took a quick peep at his watch. "I want each and every one of you to check your watches so that we'll all have the same time," he said.

"Hey, my man, how about if you ain't got no watch?" Jackie asked, as he sat down beside Billy.

Without speaking, Kenyatta nodded his head at Betty. She got up from the couch, where she had reseated herself. In a second she was back, carrying a small man's watch. She held it out to Jackie.

He took the watch from her and glanced at it. "It's a goddamn Timex," he stated to no one in particular.

"Well, I'll be damned," Betty said, speaking up for one of the few times since the men had come upstairs. "Here you give the bastard a watch and he still complains. They say you can't please a nigger. If it had been a Longine I'd bet he'd have found something wrong with that. It wouldn't have enough diamonds in it to please him or something," she finished lamely, as she noticed everyone was listening to her. It was the tension, she believed. The waiting had got to her.

"Well, I'll be damned, she can talk," Jackie stated, not angry at her for what she said. "If you have any Longines back there, I'd sure as hell appreciate one. But make sure it has at least twenty diamonds in it. I can't stand the cheap ones."

"Next time," Kenyatta said, laughing briefly. "Okay, people, everybody fix their watches. The time is," he hesitated while he rechecked his watch, "ten thirty-five. Make sure you all have that. We don't want to be off one minute." He waited until everybody had fixed their watches, then continued. "Now we get ready to move. At exactly ten forty-five, we pull up from here. We're taking two cars with us. The women along on the job will do the driving. Betty, you know what you're supposed to do. At exactly eleven o'clock you make your call. We want to catch this bastard right before he goes off duty. We know where he'll be at just about that time. Every night he takes a coffee break at about ten forty-five, so we'll have his ass gettin' in his car with his partner at just the right time."

"How about if his partner is black?" Billy asked suddenly. "I mean, I don't like cops period, but black ones I can stand a little more than I can white ones."

"He's not. It's been checked out already. I don't want to hit no black ones if I can help it, because there's not enough black ones on the force now for us to go along killin' the few that they do have," Kenyatta replied, glancing around at the group of people. Kenyatta wondered idly about Jackie. The man must be good or he wouldn't be Billy's partner, but his height was a problem. He would be easy to identify if it ever came down to that. A man with his height should be playing basketball or something, Kenyatta reflected as he studied the tall man closely. He was a drug user, too; that wasn't saying too much for him. Some damn good hit men used stuff. It was becoming a way of life for black people.

After taking one more quick glance at his watch Kenyatta stood up. "Okay, people, looks like our time has come." He pointed a finger at a slim, tiny girl. "Brenda," he said, "speeding is out tonight, you hear?" Then he added for the rest of the people's benefit, "She has a heavy foot for someone her size."

The short, black woman stood up and scowled at him. The huge natural she wore was the only thing attractive about her. On the right side of her face was a long scar that had come from a knife wound many years ago. At times when she got angry the scar seemed to glow, as it was doing now. Brenda was a hater. She hated just about everything, but white people she hated even more.

She had been raised in the South until she was old enough to leave. She worked in the cotton fields until she was fourteen, and then jumped off a truck that had brought her North to pick cherries for the cherry season. Landing on the highway with forty dollars in her purse, she had made it first to Chicago, where she worked as a prostitute until she was eighteen. Then she had come to Detroit with another girl, a dyke, but that affair had ended the night the dyke got mad and took a straight razor to her, putting the scar on her face for life.

Brenda had continued to work as a prostitute until the day Kenyatta had walked up to her and informed her that hustling in that neighborhood would have to end, unless she wanted another scar. When she had inquired as to how she was supposed to live, he had offered her a job. He was really one of the few men who had looked at her as a person instead of as a thing. He hadn't ever tried to take advantage of her. The only thing he'd ever shown her was kindness and friendship—something that had been rare indeed in her life. She had almost purred like a cat under his treatment until she, and she alone, knew that she loved him. And she would never reveal it to anyone.

"Okay, honey," Kenyatta said, holding up his hand to cut off the angry retort she was about to give. "Billy, you and Jackie ride with her. I guess I'll go in the same car as you two." He motioned to Red. "You and Big-Time will ride with Carol."

Jackie scowled at this statement. Carol was the brown-skinned girl who had been sitting on his lap. "Hey, man, why can't I ride in the car with Carol? We been gettin' along just fine tonight, so why break it up now?"

"That's the reason right there," Kenyatta answered shortly, his patience running out. The tension was getting to him, too. "This is a hard job we're going on

tonight, dangerous as hell, too. So we can't take any
chances, Jackie, none at all. You and Carol have been
becoming wonderful friends tonight, so let's wait until
we get back and you two can continue your new love
affair. But while we're on this job, I don't want no
thoughts about love interfering with what has to be
done. If she goes with you, you might just get to worrying about her. You know what I mean? You might
want her out of the way so that she might not get hurt.
Anything that would take your mind off your job is
what I don't want, so let's do it like I say, okay?"

Everybody remained silent, waiting to see what
Jackie would say. He had proven to them that he was
a man quick to anger, yet he could be reasoned with.

"The man has got a point there," Billy said quickly, not waiting for his partner to answer. "With our
driver, we ain't got to worry about nobody falling in
love," Billy added, unconcerned about how his words
would affect the woman he spoke of. Brenda was easily hurt by people referring to her looks, and Billy's
words hurt her to the core. At that instant he gained
her undying hatred.

Jackie took a quick glance at Brenda and said,
"Yeah, man, you got a point there. I don't have to
worry about no thoughts of love in my mind with our
driver." He laughed loudly, not caring about the feelings of the woman they spoke so casually about.

But Kenyatta quickly felt her hurt. He tried to come
to her rescue. "You guys act like you ain't got no
fuckin' mirrors at home. Ain't neither one of you
nothin' to write home about, so we don't have to
worry about our driver falling in love with either one
of you ugly bastards either!"

The look in Brenda's eyes as she glanced at

Kenyatta was one of thanks and of love— something she didn't realize that anyone would be able to see. Betty saw it and looked away. She felt sorry for her and had known ever since the day Brenda came that the small dark woman loved her man. It was a love that brought pity and not jealousy to the tall attractive woman who saw it.

"Well, we better be gettin' on our way if we want it to go like we've planned. Don't forget, Betty, right on the nose. That way, it shouldn't take the first police car but a minute to get there. After five minutes, make your second call. Maybe it will pull the backup car away, giving us the time it will take to finish this job right."

"Don't worry, daddy," she said as she came up and kissed her man on the cheek. "Oh, wait a minute, honey, I got something I want you to take along." She broke away from his embrace and ran into the bedroom, reappearing with a hand grenade. "Here's something that just might come in handy if you should get uptight. It's guaranteed to get you a few seconds time anyway."

He took the grenade from her. "Oh, yeah, I'm always forgettin' these little bastards. Thanks, baby." He bent over and kissed her roughly on the lips.

"Hey, my man, you got another one of those little mother hubbas? I'd sure like to have one, too," Billy said.

"Naw, man, I didn't have but two of them, and I sure ain't cuttin' the other one loose for nobody," Kenyatta answered. "Now let's get on with it. We got business to take care of."

Red gave Carol a hug as they started down the steps. "I might give Slim a run for his money tonight, honey, after we get back."

The woman laughed loudly, releasing some of the tension inside of her. "I'll be so glad to get back, Red, that I might just take on both of you!" And she prayed as she went down the stairs that she would be able to walk back up them some time that night. "Please, Lord, make me lucky enough to be one of those that comes back tonight, 'cause it sure ain't promised to none of us."

"Hey, honey, don't look so serious," Red said, patting her on her ass. "If it makes you look that serious worrying about me wantin' some, don't worry about it. I'll get in touch with my own lady tonight."

Red's attempt at humor went unheeded as they went down the stairway. Everybody was caught up in their own thoughts. There was no backing out now. Either some cops ended up dead or a bunch of young niggers would end up on the slab at the city morgue.

6

The street was dark as the two cars pulled up and parked. Kenyatta glanced up and down Greely Street before getting out. On one side of the street was a junkyard, on the other was a group of dilapidated houses waiting to be torn down. The few remaining people in them had already gotten their notices to move, but they just hadn't complied with the order yet.

Red, having jumped out of the car behind them when they parked, came up to the window. Kenyatta rolled his window down. "Go across the street and check on the gate. The lock is supposed to be fixed so that it will be open," he ordered briskly.

"Goddamn, it's turning cold," Billy stated from the backseat as they watched Red run across the street.

"We goin' cut through that junkyard?" Jackie asked, already knowing the answer, because Kenyatta had explained the getaway twice that evening before leaving the house.

"Naw, baby, not that one. We goin' run around the block and cut through the junkyard over there to get away," Kenyatta answered sarcastically.

"Okay, my man, I asked for that," Jackie answered good-naturedly, "but what about the dogs in there? I just hope your inside people have taken care of them."

Kenyatta tossed his hands in the air. "How the fuck should I know if it's taken care of or not? I arrived here with you, so I don't know. If Red don't get the shit bit out of him while he's fuckin' around over there, we'll know that everything has been taken care of. There should be a junk car waiting right inside the gate for us with the key in it. I forgot to tell you boys about that little bit of planning."

"A car!" Billy said, surprised. "I thought the broads were going to drive us away from here."

"No, not away from here." He twisted around in his seat. "Brenda, you know where I want you to park over in the projects, don't you?"

She nodded her head in agreement. "Don't worry about me, Kenyatta. I could find that spot blindfolded, honey, so don't worry about my part. You just make it over there."

Kenyatta nodded his head. "I know, baby, I ain't worried at all about you. Carol's going to follow you over there." He turned to the men in the backseat, then waited as Big-Time came walking up. Big-Time stuck his head in the window.

"Now, it's like this. Big-Time here is going to drive the car in the junkyard." He nodded to Big-Time. "Run over and check the car sittin' near the gate. The key should be in the ashtray. Make sure it starts up, and then leave the motor running if there is enough gas in it." He leaned back on the seat and continued talking. "After we make the hit, we run into the junk-yard, jump in the car, and Big-Time here will drive us to the other side of the junkyard where we jump out, climb the fence, and cross the tracks into the proj-ects. That's where the women will pick us up. This way, if there is any police after us, they should be completely thrown off course, because they won't know where the fuck we're gone. That's what's so sweet about this hit. It should go like clockwork. The getaway is perfect. You can't beat it."

Red came back from across the street as Big Time went over. Kenyatta got out of the car as he came up. "Is everything all right?"

"Fine. The dogs were still tied up, but I took care of that." He took his pistol out and unscrewed the silencer from the barrel. "I killed all four of them like you said and took the ropes off their necks. I told Big-Time to spread them out a ways so it will look like they were loose when they got shot." He hesitated, then continued, "I checked the trunk, the guns are all there."

"Good, good," Kenyatta answered quickly. "Okay, brother, ya better get on out if you're coming, we ain't got that much time left." As the two men climbed out of the backseat, Kenyatta started across the street. He waved back at Brenda. "I'll see you in a few minutes, girl. Be sure to drive careful."

The men stood on the sidewalk and watched the

cars disappear down the street. It was all a matter of time now, Billy reflected as the taillights disappeared for good.

"Come on," Red said to the men and led the way across the street. "We got to pick up our shit." Billy and Jackie fell in step behind him.

"I was under the impression we had our guns already," Billy said as he caught up with Red.

"What? Don't fool yourselves about the pistols. We ain't taking no chances on them motherfuckers gettin' away. No sirree. Whenever Kenyatta plans something, he plans the shit out of it." Red saw the look of surprise on their faces and added, "These pistols we got, brother, are our insurance pieces, that's all. You know, if we should get uptight or something like that, we'll have something to work with. But these ain't what we're going to hit them motherfuckin' cops with. Man, we got some shit that makes sure we get them bastards!" There was a note of glee in his voice.

"Hurry, hurry up," Kenyatta yelled as the men came through the junkyard gate. It was open just a crack, so that if somebody came by they wouldn't notice it.

By the time they reached the old broken-down car they were going to use, Big-Time had the trunk open. As the men took a quick look inside, Billy couldn't help but let out a yell of surprise. Inside the truck were four pump shotguns, already broken down.

"Get one," Kenyatta ordered the men. "There's plenty shells for everybody, too." He waited until each man had taken a gun and shells. "I hope everybody knows how these little bastards work," he added quickly "We ain't got much time, so watch, in case you don't know." He quickly showed the men how to load them. "Now, me and Red are going to take the dangerous side. Billy, we're crossing over to one of those empty houses, so watch which one we go into so that you don't shoot us by mistake."

He looked from one man to the other. "Billy you and Jackie will have to open fire first. I want you guys to wait until the cops have parked and got out, then cut loose on them. As soon as they duck around on the other side, if they're able, we hit them from the rear. We should be able to knock them out." He glanced at his watch, then cursed, "Goddamn, let's get set; they should be here in two more minutes." He quickly led the way back to the gate. "Keep the motor running, Big-Time. That's all I want from you. Now, as I was saying, it shouldn't take but two or three minutes to knock these cops off. In fact, we ain't even got but that much time."

The men were silent as they came out of the junkyard. "There ain't much hidin' places over here, Billy, so you and Jackie will just have to hang out in the dark. The cops won't be able to see you unless you move around. If you remain in one spot without moving, you'll take them completely by surprise." He waited until he was sure they understood. "Well, we're going to get on across the street. The police are on their way." Neither man spoke until Kenyatta and Red had crossed the street and disappeared inside the nearest dark house.

"You have to give it to that motherfucker," Jackie stated quietly as they stared into the darkness. "That bastard has really got it planned. I mean, this shit is together as far as I can see."

"Uh-huh, I can dig it," Billy replied. "You dig that house across the street," he said, pointing out the only house on the block with a light on. "I'll be willing to bet that when Betty called, she gave the police that address right over there."

"Yeah, that's got to be it. That way, the pigs will have to park damn near right in front of us," Jackie said, then nudged his partner. "Looks like the shit is about to get in the fan," he stated quickly as a car came speeding down the block, its lights shining brightly.

The police car came on swiftly, and as it approached the men it began to slow down. As soon as it stopped, the two uniformed white men inside of it started to get out, then hesitated. The one on the passenger side picked up his microphone and spoke into it for a few minutes. Unknown to the waiting men, the officer was calling for a backup car. They didn't like the looks of the dark street.

The driver of the car, Jim, didn't really care about how the street looked. His mind was on the captain who had chewed out his ass earlier that day because he had made a mistake the night before and almost shot a black detective. He was thinking at that moment how nice it would have been if he would have pumped four or five shots into the black bastard's ass. It wouldn't have been much worse if he'd shot the nigger. He'd ended up damn near getting suspended because of it.

"I don't like the looks of this," his partner said over and over again as they got out. Jim didn't even hear him. If they caught a black sonofabitch with a gun, as the call said, he'd make quick work of the nigger, he promised himself. It would be one dead black motherfucker, whether his partner liked it or not. He slammed the car door and started towards the rear of the car.

Suddenly, out of the corner of his eye, he saw some

motion where there shouldn't have been any. "What the hell?" he started to say, when flame leaped out of the darkness. A hard blow hit him in the chest and he staggered heavily. As he reeled back against the car, the night seemed to explode with fire. He clawed at his holster, but it was a feeble effort. Another staggering blow sent him down to his knees, and before he could recover he felt the pavement come up and smash him in the face.

His partner heard the first shot and swore out loud. Then the night lit up for him as he stared through the windows of the car at the gun flashes coming out of the darkness. He glanced up and down the street frantically. He saw the red lights coming down the street and knew at once that it was their backup squad coming to help them. He let out a sigh of relief, even though he realized at once that it was too late for his partner. Then suddenly a blow struck him in the back and slammed him against the car door. He jerked at the doorknob, trying to reenter the car. Somehow he managed to get the door open, but before he could get into the car, another staggering blow caught him in the middle of his back. He never knew when he hit the sidewalk because he was dead on his feet.

The second police car came to a halt instantly beside the parked one. The black and white policemen inside the car looked at each other, stunned. Before the driver could make up his mind, flame came blasting out of the darkness towards them. The shots took out the window, shattering it and covering the two men with glass. Neither man was hurt, though each was so frightened that fear kept them huddled down on the seat. The officer on the passenger side managed to get on the radio and send out a frantic call.

As the officers stayed huddled on the seat, neither one saw the two men come out of the condemned house and move nearer to the car. Neither noticed the man pulling the small round-shaped ball from his pocket and remove the pin. Neither saw the thing make an arc in the air until suddenly they felt the car lifted off the ground as they were hurled towards death. They both died with neither man ever realizing how. The few people living inside the condemned houses hadn't bothered to come outside to see what the gunshots were all about. They stayed in their homes, waiting out the noise of death and hoping against hope that none of the shots would hit them. Even though they lived in poverty and despair, none wanted to give up their meager existence of poor food and hopeless dreams.

Red was the first one across the street. Then Kenyatta walked across, examining the body of the policeman in the street to make sure he was dead. As the body made a final jerk, he aimed his shotgun at the man and pulled the trigger. The body jumped from the weight of the blow. Kenyatta continued to walk, only widening his steps. When he entered the junkyard, he closed the gate behind him, making sure it was locked.

The men inside the waiting car watched their leader take his time. "Goddamn, that man has the nerve of ten fools," Red said as he waited impatiently for him.

Big-Time raced the motor. "I heard the shootin'. Did everything go like planned?" he asked, trying to fight down the panic inside him. He could hardly keep from putting the car in gear and racing away from there. He wanted to let the window down and yell for Kenyatta to come the fuck on. He wanted to drive away and leave Kenyatta's slow-moving ass. All these things and more flashed through his mind, but he fought down the panic.

Billy and Jackie were the professional ones, but they too felt the need for speed. It didn't make sense wasting time. The job was over and now they needed to get away. Why was he moving so slow? You didn't shoot cops every day, and if you ever did, you had better make quick tracks. Billy started to roll down his window and tell Kenyatta to bring his black ass on, but seeing the fear in the other two men in the front seat made him hesitate. If they were that frightened and showed it, how was he looking? He glanced over at Jackie. Yes, Jackie was nervous, but he didn't reveal his impatience. He was slowly lighting a cigarette. Billy decided to follow his example, removing his pack and lighting up.

When Kenyatta finally reached the car, he pushed his pack of smokes up towards the front seat and held them. "Here, my man, you might as well take a smoke before we leave," he said sarcastically.

Before the words were out of his mouth, Big-Time had the car in gear and was speeding away. "Hey, my man," Billy yelled, "slow this motherfucker down. We don't want to run into anything now!"

"He's telling you right," Kenyatta added from his seat in front. "Slow this motherfucker down," he yelled as Big-Time almost hit another junked car parked in the aisle. In the next instant they went down an aisle that was blocked. As Big-Time tried to back out, he ran into another parked car. The man muttered under his breath and put the car in gear and pulled forward. As soon as he got the car straightened out, he began backing up again. This time he made it back to the aisle they had started from. He turned around and tried another one. This too was piled up and blocked by other junks.

"Goddamn it, Kenyatta, you planned everything but which way to take us where we're supposed to go," Jackie shouted from the rear seat.

"Yeah, man, but it ain't no big thing. It shouldn't be no big problem gettin' out of here," he stated with more assurance than he felt. As Big-Time picked another dead end the men began to worry.

"Maybe we had better get out and walk," Billy said. "We ain't got that much time. If he keeps fuckin' around, police are going to be swarming all over this motherfucker!"

Even Kenyatta realized the truth in his words. They had time, but they didn't have that much time. If they didn't hurry up, the junkyard could turn into a trap. Once the police realized that they had gone through it, it would be covered from front to back.

"Man, take your time and look where you're going," Kenyatta ordered.

"If I could only turn on the lights for a minute or two," Big-Time whined, "I could see what I'm doing."

"Hey man, let me under that steering wheel," Billy growled. "We can't have no lights, ignorant-ass motherfucker! Where's your brains, nigger? In your ass?" His temper was rising as he began to realize that Big-Time's driving could get them busted.

"Here, here, here," Kenyatta yelled over and over again. He didn't want the men to panic. That was the last thing he needed. "You guys just stay cool, everything is going to be all right. Make a right turn, boy," he ordered sharply. "I been over this yard a dozen times, and I know the way out. It just looks funny at night without any lights on. Turn left at the next corner—that's right. This road should lead us right to the back fence."

As Big-Time noticed an open road in front of him, he began to speed up again. "Slow this motherfucker down," Kenyatta ordered, then pulled out his pistol. "If I have to tell you again, I'm going to blow your shit out!" He cocked the pistol in Big-Time's face.

At the sight of the cocked pistol, Big-Time began to shake all over. He swerved off the road and struck another parked car. The speed of the moving car slammed the men in front against the dashboard. The men in the back came out better.

Billy cursed loudly as he spit blood from a cut lip. Red pulled back, bleeding from a large cut on his temple. Kenyatta came out a little better. He only hurt his arm, but his temper was at the breaking point.

As the men settled back in the car, Big-Time sat behind the steering wheel crying like a child. "I couldn't help it, I just couldn't help it, Kenyatta. You shouldn't have pointed the gun at me." Real tears began to roll down his cheeks as he cried louder.

In disgust Kenyatta raised the pistol and pointed it at the man's head. "This is the reason I brought your punk ass along, Big-Time. I wanted to see if you had any nuts. Now I see you ain't nothing but pure pussy, man. Pure pussy!" He raised the pistol and pulled the trigger.

"Motherfucker," Jackie stated, then turned to his partner. "Billy, wipe everything off back here, man. Make sure we don't leave any prints in this ride."

Billy was staring straight ahead at Kenyatta. The sight of Big-Time slumped over the wheel didn't frighten him, but it surprised the hell out of him.

"Yeah, man, we better clean up good."

In the front seat, Kenyatta had started to get out, then he saw what they were doing in the back and started to do the same thing in front. "Make sure you wipe up everything, Red," he ordered sharply.

Red jumped to it, wiping everything in sight. The coldblooded murder had shaken him to his roots.

Kenyatta glanced up as everyone came out of the car. "The shotguns are just excess baggage," he yelled, "so just make sure they're clean of prints and dump them in the ride."

"We got to move," Billy said under his breath as he quickly rewiped his weapon. "We done wasted too much fuckin' time in this junkyard."

"I know just what you mean," Jackie replied quickly, as he tossed his gun on the seat. "Let's make tracks."

"Don't worry, we still got plenty of time," Kenyatta stated coldly as he led the way towards the rear of the junkyard. The sound of sirens could be heard in the distance as the men hurried.

"Shit!" Billy cursed as he stepped into a mud puddle. "How much farther have we got to go?" The sound of men pulling their feet out of sucking mud could be heard. Finally in the distance they could see the tall wire fence.

When they reached the fence, Kenyatta led the way along it, looking for a certain spot, and he finally found what he was looking for. The wire had been cut, and underneath the fence someone had placed cardboard so that the men could slip under it without getting too dirty. Kenyatta was the first one under and, after he got to the other side, he held the wire up slightly so that the rest of the men wouldn't have too much trouble. After they were all across he removed the cardboard and carried it down the railroad tracks until they were quite a distance from where they had crossed over. Not until then did he toss the cardboard away.

There was no light anywhere around the tracks and Billy wondered how Kenyatta could see where they were to go. But just as the thought was flashing through his mind, Kenyatta left the tracks and started making his way through some weeds. The men followed behind him quietly. Suddenly, out of the darkness, they could see buildings.

Before the men could realize where they were headed they were on pavement. Then the sight of a cigarette glowing inside a parked car filled them with joy. They had made it!

7

The pitch-black street was now illuminated by the arrival of a great many police cars. Detective Benson and his partner, Ryan, moved around the death scene slowly, trying to get a fix on what had happened. Four policemen were dead, and somebody was going to have to pay for it.

Somehow the newspapers got word of the killings, and soon radio and even television personnel began to arrive. Detective Ryan stared at the crowd of people angrily. How the hell were they supposed to work, he wondered, with so many fucking people in the way?

A newspaperman from one of the daily papers came bearing down on him. "Hey, Ryan," the man called out, "wait up. I just want a few words with you."

Ryan stopped and waited patiently for the man to catch up. "What can I do for you?" Ryan inquired as the man came abreast of them.

"You can give me a rundown on just what happened out here tonight. Jesus Christ, it's like a butcher shop!"

Benson put his hand over his mouth and turned away to cover up the smile that was about to break through. "I'll be right back," he said to his partner and walked across the street to the junkyard. He examined the gate on the closed yard, then trained his flashlight through the wire gate. It picked up the body of a dog, lying on its side. He examined the dog closely, then yelled out to his partner, "Hey, Ryan, you better come on over here. I think I might have found something."

His voice carried to quite a few people, and by the time Ryan reached him there were four other detectives standing around waiting to see what he had come up with. He cut on his light and showed his partner the dead dog. Other flashlights came on, and soon the front of the yard was flooded with light. The sight of other dead dogs was picked up.

"The fuckin' yard's full of dead dogs," someone in the crowd murmured loudly.

"Somebody get a crowbar so we can get in this fuckin' place," a huge red-faced man wearing a dark suit ordered sharply.

In a matter of minutes the gate was forced open and the detectives started through "Somebody keep them goddamn newspaper people out of here," the same huge man ordered. His voice was deep and carried all the way across the yard. The newspaperman walking beside Ryan growled in his ear, "Who the hell is that big lard-ass bastard?"

Ryan stopped in his tracks and glared at the man. "That happens to be the Chief of Homicide, mister, and he has a job to do just like I have. So if you don't mind, give me a break, okay?"

Before the man could answer, Ryan walked away from him and joined Benson. "How the hell did you get away from your shadow?" Benson asked.

"Bullshit, that's all it is. Why somebody didn't set up a roadblock and cut off all those big-nose bastards I don't know. They get in the fuckin' way so that nobody can do their job. Then when you don't come right out and solve a murder, they're the first ones to jump down your fuckin' back. They kill you in the papers, but wait until you run into one of the bastards out here on a job. Then they try and treat you like a long-lost brother."

Benson shrugged his shoulders. "Well, I wouldn't know about all that. They overlook me most of the time. I guess they think I'm just here for decoration or something."

Ryan grinned at his friend and partner. "Yeah, I know, you have it tough. I didn't see you fightin' off no fuckin' newspapermen though. When you have to do that, that's when your trouble starts."

"Yeah, I know," Benson answered quickly, "that's why my heart bleeds for you. You have so much trouble, but that's what happens when you become famous."

Ryan moved one of the dogs slightly with his foot. "These bastards have been shot," he stated loudly, as he bent down and examined the dogs closer.

"Man, you know this fuckin' midnight shift is gettin' to be too damn busy," Benson stated while he waited for Ryan to finish examining the dog.

Ryan straightened up. "I guess you noticed who one of the policemen out there was, didn't you?"

"I haven't lost my eyesight yet. Of course I noticed the guy. It's a shame it had to happen, no matter how I felt about him. He was still a police officer," Benson replied, studying his partner closely.

"Yeah, I know what you mean," Ryan replied quickly, too quickly to suit Benson. "This shit has got to be solved, and solved quickly. We can't let no bastards run around knocking off cops whenever they feel like it. If this shit keeps up, we won't have a police department. This makes eight policemen who have been set up. And believe me, this was definitely a setup."

Benson nodded his head as he remembered the other unsolved police murders. "Yeah, it's gettin' out of hand, there's no doubt about that."

As the night wore on, the men working became angrier. The newspapermen and television crews were in the way everywhere the detectives turned, until tempers were ready to flare.

Ryan and Benson worked on in silence inside the junkyard. It was late when the other body was discovered. By then the owner of the junkyard had shown up and turned on the lights. While the men searched, the body of one of the men who worked around the yard was also found. It had been piled in behind some cars that were waiting to be mashed up. At the discovery of this body, the chief of police tossed his hands in the air and walked out of the yard. His cursing could be heard clear across the yard.

The men worked on and on. This was above all a cop-killing and they wanted some answers. Daybreak found them still searching through the piles of junk cars, looking for any sort of clue. The guns had been found in the rear of the old car and rushed to the police lab in hopes that fingerprints could be gotten off of them.

Benson came walking slowly up the dirt road. He glanced over at the tired detective tugging along beside him. Ryan was walking with his head down, ignoring the deep puddles of mud they came to. Both detectives were deep in thought, neither man bothering to break the silence. Cold-blooded murder like this didn't make any kind of sense to Benson, and he prayed quietly that they would catch the men responsible as soon as possible.

"Well, what do you think?" Ryan asked as he came up alongside his friend.

"Think! I don't even bother to do such a thing. It goes against the grain when you come up against something like this. The people who are responsible for this must be mad. I mean, people just don't go around killing wholesale like this. What's the reason behind it? It's senseless, as far as I can see." Benson dropped his head. What could he say? As far as he could see, they were right back where they started, yet they had six new deaths on their hands. Every one of the people had been murdered by the same bunch of people. They knew too that four men had gone under the fence at the rear of the yard, but that evidence wasn't strong enough to shed any light on who was responsible. They couldn't even tell if the black man found in the car was in on it or a witness who happened to be at the wrong place at the wrong time.

As the two officers came out of the gate they saw the police commissioner standing in front, giving an interview to the television men. They walked past the group and went on towards their unmarked car. They climbed in and just sat there, each man deep in his own thoughts. Both men were tired from the long night's work, prowling in and out of the old cars, searching for something and not sure what.

"Well, Ryan, what do we do from here?" Benson asked quietly.

"Your guess is as good as mine," Ryan answered just as softly. "I could say let's go down in the ghettos and shake up some asses, but where would we start?"

"That would at least give us some kind of work. Let's check with some informers. Maybe something will break that way," Benson offered, wanting to do something other than just sit there idly.

Ryan started up the motor and pulled away. "Well, at least that will give us something to go on," he replied, driving slowly away from the spot of so much violence.

The men rode in silence. The night had been too much for both of them. Each man was used to violence, but not on such a large scale.

"You know," Benson finally said, "what we need to do, Ryan, is get ahold of some drug addicts. Maybe one of them knows something." He glanced over at his partner to see how he was taking the idea.

Ryan smiled to himself. "Yeah, just like we did on that other case where we didn't get nowhere. But you're right about that. We need somebody to break this case open for us, and a hype is likely to talk before anybody else."

"How about your buddy over in narco? You think we could ride with them for a while and question some of the junkies they knock over?"

"That's an idea," Ryan replied. "But you know my

friend's on the afternoon shift, so we'd have to work a lot of hours on our own time."

"I don't give a shit as long as we get a break on these murders, Ryan. That's all I'm concerned about."

Ryan smiled in the dark. Benson was the first black man he had ever worked with. Before Benson came on the shift with him he'd had his doubts about whether or not it would work. Now they had reached such a point that he wouldn't feel right working with anybody else. If they took Benson away from him now, he would have big trouble trying to readjust to another man. For some reason the two men just clicked together. It had reached the point where they even took their wives out together. Of course people stared at the black and white couples, but the men were past the stage where looks bothered them.

"Let's go in and finish up whatever paperwork we have, then take the rest of the fuckin' night off. I'll give the boss an idea of what we're going to do so he'll know we're working damn near a double shift. Maybe he'll switch us over to the afternoon. That way, we won't have to burn the candle at both ends," Ryan stated as he drove towards the freeway. He didn't have to wait for his partner's okay. The men understood each other too well for that.

It was late next day when they came in. Ryan glanced up from his desk as Benson strolled over. "How the hell are you, Joe?" Benson asked in a joking manner. The two men grinned. "How did the chief like your idea?"

"My idea shit," Ryan replied. "I told him it was both of our fuckin' ideas, so he said to punch in. We can pick up some overtime. He doesn't want us knocking our asses off on free time. Just as long as we get the fuckin' case solved, he doesn't give a shit how much overtime we put in."

"That sounds all right. How did the boys down in narco take to the idea of us riding along with them?" Benson inquired as he picked up a file from the desk and glanced through it.

Ryan grinned up at him. "It's not even necessary for us to ride out. They're going to call us down to interrogate whatever addicts they bring in. There's a couple of junkies on ice right now, waiting for us to see them. I was just waiting for you to come along. I figured you'd get plenty of rest and come in when you were ready."

"Hey, that's what I'd call sharp work, if I was in any kind of position to call it anything, Ryan. Where are we going to talk to our little pigeons? Up here or downstairs?"

"We might as well take the elevator down to the ninth floor where the boys are. It will save us a lot of trouble," Ryan answered as he got up from his desk. "You know, the chances are small that we'll come in contact with a junkie who really knows anything about this shit. This seems like it's being done by someone who has some kind of plan. Maybe one of the militant organizations, you know. That's what I'm thinking our problem is. We don't know what fuckin' militant group is trying to clean the streets up!"

"Clean the streets up? Clean them up of what? Police?" Benson asked, incredulous.

As his partner glared down at him, Ryan got up from behind his desk and came around it. "Well, our arguing won't solve our problem, so let's get downstairs and rap to a few of our clients."

Benson shrugged his shoulders in despair. "I'm trying to still make something out of your idea, Ryan. I definitely agree with you on a militant organization being behind this shit. It makes sense of some sort. I mean, this is not being done by just some guy out in the street who hates cops. It's more than one man involved, so it makes sense that an organization is the key. But which one?"

"We don't have that yet, but if we fuck around and dig deep enough, buddy, I think we can come up with something," Ryan stated as he led the way towards the elevator. The men rode downstairs in silence.

They spoke to the guard on the ninth floor, then waited until the man went in the rear where the prisoners were held. There was a large steel door separating the guards from the prisoners. On one side was an enclosed room with wire mesh that the prisoner had to talk through whenever his lawyer came up to see him. This room was not for visitors.

In a matter of minutes the guard was back. He had to wait until his partner opened the door from the inside, allowing him to come into the large room where the guards sat at their desks. None of the guards were armed, and the two detectives had to check their weapons before the guards would allow them to take the prisoner down the corridor to one of the empty interrogation rooms.

The prisoner, short, brown-skinned, and with a dirty beard, followed along behind the guard. The man was silent, watching the developments quietly. He waited until the two detectives had entered the room and closed the door before saying anything.

"What's the deal, man?" he inquired in a cold voice, staring from one officer to the other.

"We just want to have a few words with you," Ryan

said softly. "If you want to help yourself, you can."

The man shrugged his shoulders. "I don't know anybody who sells drugs, mack. So it's a waste of your time bugging me about pushers, 'cause I don't give a fuck how long you keep me down here, you ain't goin' make no fuckin' snitch out of me."

Benson let out a soft laugh. "Did you hear anybody ask you about any pushers?" He glanced down at the brown folder that Ryan had been carrying. "Johnson, Edward Johnson. That's your real name, isn't it?"

The black man glanced over at Benson as if he was seeing him for the first time. "Ain't that what they got down there?"

Seeing that the man was going to be hostile, Ryan spoke up. "Have a seat, Johnson. Would you care for a smoke?"

The man ignored the outstretched pack of cigarettes and reached over and removed a butt out of the ashtray to light up. The men got the message at once. This one was going to be hard to get along with.

"Now, Johnson," Ryan began again, trying to bridge the gap, "we didn't have you brought in here to bug you. We just want to ask you a few questions."

Johnson stared at the policeman as though he was something from another world. "Listen, mack," he said in that cold, matter-of-fact voice of his, "I know what you guys think about dope fiends, but it ain't like that with all of us. Every addict you pick up ain't no informer, so quit wasting your time and mine. I ain't got nothing to say to you. I wouldn't give you motherfuckers the time of day. Can you dig it?"

"It looks as if this guy wants to spend the whole seventy-two hours in the lockup, don't it?" Benson said to his partner, ignoring the man.

Johnson spit on the floor. "I ain't spending a motherfuckin' thing nowhere, mack. I'm bailing out of this dump today. I was just waiting to see the detectives. You guys picked me up on a meatball. I ain't robbed nobody, so you ain't got no case on me. Now, if you're finished with me, I'll go on back and wait for my lawyer to call me out."

Benson caught his partner's eye and Ryan nodded slowly. "Hey, Dep," Benson called out, "get this character out of here." He turned his back on the prisoner. Guys like him gave Benson the ass. He could hardly keep from kicking the shit out of the man. He hated them, every fucking one of the smart-ass bastards that came off the streets with that attitude.

When the guard arrived, Benson said, "Take this one back and bring us the other guy."

Johnson walked out without saying anything to the two detectives. He sneered at the deputy as he fell in step. "My lawyer ain't out there nowhere, is he?" he inquired, loud enough for the two detectives to hear.

"Some of them are like that," Ryan said, tossing his hands in the air. "Maybe the other one won't be so hard."

The detectives studied the folder of the other prisoner. "Brown, James Brown. The guy has got a famous name anyway," Ryan said.

The other guard came forward, leading a tall, dark-complexioned man who looked to be in his early forties. The man came in bent over, and it was easy to see that he was sick. He was going through the withdrawal symptoms of true drug addiction. His nose was running, and tears ran out of his eyes as big as pennies.

"Hey, man," he said as he took the seat offered him,

"why you guys rousing me like this? I wasn't doing nothing but going down the street to cop, then these cops jump out on me and said I knocked off a drugstore. I wasn't even near the damn place, man."

"We know, Brown; we're going to help you too, if you give us a little help," Ryan said softly, as he watched the man's hands shake. "Yeah, Brown, if you help us, you'll be on your way home in the next hour."

The mention of going home changed the man's features. It was like the sun breaking through on a rainy day. He even managed to smile slightly. "Man, if I can help you, I'll do whatever I can."

"Good, but don't give us no shit, hear?" Benson said harshly, leaning on the man and playing the role of the tough cop.

The man glanced over his shoulder at Benson. "Hey, man, why you want to give me a hard time? I ain't giving you guys no problem, am I?"

"Who's your pusher?" Ryan asked sharply, not giving the man time to set himself.

Brown began to shift around in the chair, and he mumbled a name under his breath. "It's Little Dave," he said louder when Benson nudged him in the back.

"How does Little Dave sell his stuff? Does he deliver, or do you go to his house?" Ryan asked quickly.

"Naw, man," Brown answered slowly, glancing around. "Hey man, this shit ain't going no further, is it? A guy can get killed real quick for saying as much as I've said already."

"Don't worry about it, James. It ain't going no damn further than this room. We just want to see if you're going to act nice or be an asshole," Ryan replied.

"How do you get your mess from him?" Benson asked sharply. "You got the guy's address?"

"Naw, man, he comes up on the corner every day at the same time, two o'clock, you dig. If you want to cop, you had better be up there by then."

For the next half an hour they talked to the man, writing down information that would help the narcotics department but wouldn't help them.

Finally Benson put forth the question that they had been building up to. "Who the hell are these guys, or what's the name of this gang of punks who think they can knock off all the white cops in the city, James? I know you've heard something about it, man, so level with us on it."

Brown shook his head. "I've heard guys talk about it, man, but they didn't know what the hell was going on, you know what I mean? Guys get together and shit like this comes up, but nobody downtown knows the names of the people responsible for it. I'm telling you the real, man, 'cause if I knew, I'd tell you. It don't do me no good for these guys to make the streets so hot. I can't walk down them." Brown glanced from one officer to the other one. "This is the truth, man. I done gave you guys my pusher's name, so you know I'd gladly tell you the name of whoever these punks were."

The two officers glanced at each other, sure the man was telling them the truth. "Listen, man," Brown began, his voice holding a whining note, "if you guys kick me out on the bricks, I'll tell you what I'll do. I'll keep my ears open for you. Really man, give me a number and the first time I hear something dealing with this shit, I'll get in touch with you guys. I know it would be a feather in your caps to bust this one wide open, so give me a break. I can't help you from in here, but outside, you never know. These kind of things have a way of being talked about. You know

what I mean?" He glanced from one officer to the
other one, hoping that his plea didn't fall on deaf ears.
"I mean it, guys, really I do. It don't make sense keeping me in here for nothing. I'm sick now. Oh man,
this time tomorrow I'll be climbing the walls!"

Ryan caught his partner's eye. Benson gave him a
nod. It was okay with him; they could use an informer
in the streets. "Listen Brown, if we cut you loose,
don't give us no shit, 'cause we can have you picked
up any fuckin' time we feel like it. Now, if we do free
you, we want to hear something from you, you understand? By this time next week if we ain't heard from
you, your ass has had it. Do I make myself clear?"
Ryan said to the shaking man.

"I hear you, man; you mean you're really goin' kick
me out the front door and let me go?" He couldn't
believe his luck. He watched Ryan write down a number, then push it across to him. "This is our number.
I'm Ryan, that's Benson. You better be in touch with
one of us by this time next week or you won't be so
lucky next time. We'll let your ass rot in here if you
give us a snow job on this shit!"

Ryan turned to his partner. "You want to go up front
and clear this matter up so that Brown can go home?"

Benson glanced down at Brown. "Yeah, I'll do it
this time, but this bastard better produce for us," he
said as he started for the door.

Brown followed him with his eyes. He still couldn't
believe his luck. These two cops were heavy bastards
at that. It might pay off in the long run for him to
work for them. Whenever he got busted on some
chicken-shit case, all he'd have to do would be give
them a ring and they could spring him.

"You know," Brown began, trying to find out just

how far he could go with these guys, "if I should help you guys out, maybe sometime I'd need a favor out of you, you know what I mean?" he inquired in that whining voice of his.

Ryan stared at the junkie. "Yeah, I know what you mean," he said, getting sick of the sight of him. Informers had a way of doing that to him. For some reason, he ended up hating every one of them that he did business with. "You mean that if you get busted for something small you want us to come to your rescue, huh?" Ryan asked sharply.

Brown couldn't look him in the eye. "I mean something like that. If I help you guys through this one, I'd feel like you owe me a favor, 'cause this is a big one, ain't it?"

For a minute Ryan hesitated, then said slowly, "Yeah it's a big one all right." What difference did it make if he pulled some strings and got the man out of jail on some petty charge? If the man helped break this murder case it would sure in the hell be worth it. "Yeah, Brown, you get me some information on who's responsible for these cop killings and I'll surely owe you some favors."

Knowing that he would soon be going home made a new man out of Brown. He smiled now, as he talked to the detective. "You got the right boy here, Mr. Ryan. Yes siree, when James Brown says he's goin' do somethin', man, you can bet your last dollar he's goin' do it."

As he listened to the man talk, Ryan really believed him. The only reason Brown didn't help them would be because he couldn't find out anything. But if the man was sincere, he should hear something in the streets that would help them.

Benson came back in the room. "It's all taken care of. The paperwork will take a few minutes, then this guy can walk."

"Our boy Brown here says he's going to help us bust this case wide open. All he wants for this help is a little favor every now and then," Ryan stated quietly.

"Uh huh," Benson said and leaned on the desk. "Hey, Brown, did you by any chance know anything about this guy Jo-Jo that got offed with his wife and kid? I hear the guy was dealing, so you should have heard something about it," Benson asked quietly.

"Naw, man, it wasn't downtown, was it? I ain't heard a word about it. If it don't go down around John R, or Brush, it's out of my district, you know what I mean? That's why I say it was out of my hangout, 'cause I ain't never heard of this guy. You say he was dealing, well it sure wasn't downtown."

"Maybe these guys who are knockin' off these cops are out of your district too. If that's the case, you won't be much help to us after all, Brown," Ryan stated quietly, feeling the man out.

"Naw, man, this is different. This thing is big. Everybody in the city is talking about it. I mean, four cops get knocked off at the same time, this is something too big to stay out in the boondocks. It's got to be let out. I just can't believe whoever done it will stay in the shadows. Somebody is going to talk, and I promise you guys, I'll be listening."

Benson glared at him. "I promise you that you'd better be listening, too," he said, just as the deputy knocked on the door.

The two detectives watched their bird go out, each one hoping that their long shot would pay off.

8

The apartment was still dark when Carol got up and pulled back the drapes. The sun came in, flooding the room with the morning's rays. Jackie remained stretched out on the bed, watching her as she moved about the room. She wasn't a beauty, but she had a personality, and that's what counted in his book. Ever since he had met the woman, he had begun to become involved with her. Their relationship was the cause of his getting so involved with Kenyatta—a relationship that he wasn't too happy about.

"You think Billy is up yet?" she asked, climbing across the bed and kissing him on the cheek.

Jackie grinned, "I could care less if Billy is up or

not. Why are you worried about Billy this morning?"

"I was going to fix some breakfast for everybody, honey. You want three eggs or four?" He watched her try to put her hand behind her back in a subconscious move. Since she only had three fingers on her right hand, she was self-conscious about it.

Jackie pulled her arm from around her back and kissed her deformed hand. She blushed as she tried to pull away.

"Please, honey, don't do that," she begged as she struggled with him. "You know I'm embarrassed when you do that."

"Fuck that shit," he growled. "I want you to stop hiding your hand behind your back. When you stop hiding it, I'll stop embarrassing you."

Carol smiled down at him. "Okay, Jack in the bean stack, I dig where you're coming from. Now, how about us gettin' up and havin' some food?"

Jackie let her go reluctantly. He watched her walk across the floor until she went into the living room. He listened and heard the exchange between her and Billy. Yeah, he told himself, it was time to get up. Maybe he'd take in a show or something. The thought of a movie made him remember the shape of his bankroll. Working with Kenyatta didn't put any money in their pockets, that was for sure. That dedication shit was for the birds. Fuck killing all the dope men in the city. He could care less about who sold dope. It would be good to knock them off for their bread, though. That was what he'd been waiting for. That and when Kenyatta finally got his hands on that list he was always talking about so they could make a hit on the big men. Any big man should be loaded with dough. They had to keep money around the house in big stacks because it came in that way. Nobody could run to the bank with ten grand every day and not get busted for it. No, Kenyatta might not be worried about the money, but he and Billy sure were. They had gotten in so tight with Kenyatta that he would send them out on a job and put one of them in charge. He knew now from experience that they were pros.

"Come on, nigger, get your long ass out of that bed," Billy yelled from the doorway. "Carol must be wearing your ass out, man." Billy silently watched Jackie climb out of the bed. Carol was good for the man, Billy thought as he studied his partner. She was the first girl he had ever known Jackie to allow to stay with him. He had let some women stay overnight, but after that he sent them on their way. Carol, for some reason, had touched that spot inside of the big man.

"Come on in, brother," Jackie called out as he put on his pants. "Carol's gettin' us some grub together, man. Why don't you find yourself a seat, on the bed there if you want to. Just push that shit out of your way." For some reason he felt good this morning. He generally got up wanting some dope, but this morning he didn't care for the stuff. As he thought about it, he realized that it had been three or four days since he had wanted a snort in the morning. Ever since Carol came along, actually. He told Billy this.

"Yeah, man, I noticed the fact that you wasn't blowing as much as you had been," Billy replied quickly. "It's showing up on you too. You're gaining back some of that weight you were losing, my man."

Jackie grinned over at his partner. "Yeah, man, she seems to be agreeable to my system, don't she?" Both men laughed together, then Jackie continued, "I been thinkin', Billy. We goin' have to knock off something, brother. Our rent is coming due, and I don't have my share of the bread."

"Shit, I don't have mine either," Billy replied evenly. "But we'll find something to knock over before then. I'm sure of it."

"Yeah, but I don't want to have to knock off some poor bastard for petty change; I want the next job to be big enough so that we won't have to work for quite a while."

Billy shook his head in agreement. "Why you think we been wasting our time buttering up Kenyatta's mad ass for? Not for the joy of it, I hope," he replied shortly. "Now that we got the guy's faith, he'll loan us the men we need to knock off that food-stamp place."

"I hope you're right about that," Jackie replied. "I know you and Kenyatta have been talking, but has he said anything about it?"

"Yeah, baby boy, he sure has. You know he needs that ten grand to pay for that list he wants so bad. Damn, that's a lot of money for just a gang of names, but he's really going to set the cash out. So he wants up on a big job. We've talked about it even to the point of his helping plan the thing. You know, that big black bastard can really plan something whenever he sets his mind to it," Billy stated, removing his cigarettes and lighting one.

"Be sure to use the ashtray, nigger. I don't want my room like yours," Jackie said good-naturedly.

"You know, partner, if the disorder of my room disturbs you, all you have to do is loan me Carol for a little while. I'm sure she can straighten out that small matter."

"No thanks, Billy. She ain't no maid. When you take off this big caper, try hiring you a good maid. It shouldn't be too hard if your buck is right."

"Hey, in there! You guys goin' talk all morning or eat?" Carol called out from the dining room.

Both men got up quickly and went towards the kitchen. Carol had taken the time to set the dining room table for them. They both smiled. They weren't used to getting such wonderful treatment.

The breakfast consisted of eggs and bacon, plus some toast. She had steaming hot coffee waiting for them too. The two men ate in silence, enjoying the well-prepared food. Carol watched them eat, happy to be wanted. She enjoyed the company of these men who got along so well.

"Are you going over to Kenyatta's today?" she inquired as the men washed down their food with the hot coffee.

Neither man answered her right off. Jackie glanced over at Billy and waited for him to reply. "Well," Carol asked, "has the cat got both of your tongues?"

"What do you think about it, Jackie?" Billy asked, still undecided.

"It's not what I think. It's what kind of shape we're in. I think we had better go over and get something together with the man. I mean, I'm down to my last ten-dollar bill, Billy. I don't know how you're fixed for cash, but my bankroll is finished."

Billy nodded his head in agreement. "It's kind of bad then. I'm damn near in the same shape. I got about twenty-five dollars, but it ain't goin' last no time." He pushed back from the table. "I'd say we run over and talk to him about that deal we were kickin' around."

"Jackie, I got a few dollars, honey," Carol stated softly, so that he had to almost lean over to hear what she said.

"What?" he exclaimed, but before she repeated herself he continued, proving that he had heard what she said after all. "Naw, baby, I don't want to take your chump change. In fact, I don't really need it, Carol. I'm going to get some cash together real soon, but if I should get up tight, I'll let you know." He smiled at her, letting her know that he appreciated the offer.

"Damn," Billy exclaimed, stretching out on the couch, "that food really hit the spot. I'm so full I can hardly move. We goin' have to start havin' you get it together for us more often, Carol." He opened up his belt to give his stomach room. "I shouldn't have drunk all that damn coffee. I'm not used to eating a big breakfast, you know."

"Jackie," she called out. "When ya go over to Kenyatta's, can I go too? I don't feel like going home and sittin' around, so I might as well get out into the streets with you guys." She knew that Jackie was actually jealous of the time she spent at Kenyatta's club, but she had been a member for over a year now, and as she told him, she wasn't about to give it up. She believed in what the man was doing in trying to clean up the ghettos of dope pushers and pimps. No other organization was really doing anything and she could see the results of Kenyatta's work. He had cleaned the streets of whores, since the pimps had moved their girls. It had been too much trouble fighting with Kenyatta's dedicated men. They were fools, so the pimps thought. But dangerous fools.

With his stomach protruding further than necessary, Jackie came in the front room and flopped down in a chair. "We might as well get on over there and lay it down to Kenyatta, man, 'cause we got to have the bread."

Billy let out a sigh, then pushed up from the chair. "Let's get on with it then," he stated, tightening his belt.

"Damn, when you make up your mind to go, you don't waste any time, do you?" Jackie replied. "Hey, Carol, if you don't want to get left behind, you better shake a leg. We gettin' ready to pull up, honey."

Before the words were out of his mouth, Carol came running out of the bedroom. "I'm ready, honey; I was just straightening up things." She was smiling brightly.

Jackie took her arm and led her out of the apartment. Billy followed behind, closing the door and locking it. They piled in the car, with Billy behind the steering wheel. When they reached Kenyatta's club, there was another group of men loitering outside. This time they were recognized by a few of the men. Names were mentioned and one man spoke to Carol, bringing a scowl to Jackie's face. The girl at the desk was a different one this time, but Billy and Jackie still knew her. They walked past the desk and knocked on the door.

"Come on in," Kenyatta called out. The small group of people went in, closing the door behind them. No one was in the office except Kenyatta's woman and him. "What's happening, baby?" Kenyatta said from behind the desk, where he was going over a diagram.

"I got something here you guys might be interested in," he said as they came up. He stood up and showed them the blueprint he had unfolded on his desk. It was the layout of the food-stamp building.

Billy smiled broadly. "I got to give you credit, Kenyatta. You don't waste any time, man. That's what we came over to talk to you about, and you're already on the case."

Kenyatta smiled back at the men, revealing beautiful, evenly-spaced teeth. "When it comes to big cash, man, I can't afford to waste time. I need money just like you do. This joint here takes plenty of that shit to run, plus my farm." He grinned as the men looked surprised. "Yeah, brother, I got a farm. Where do you think I train my people at? Not in this motherfucker, I hope."

"What kind of fuckin' farm?" Billy asked, not really believing Kenyatta yet.

"Just an ordinary farm, brother. Out in what you city boys would call a rural area, out around Fourteen Mile Road. We ain't got but twenty acres of good farming land, but it's ours. We go out and picnic at times, ride the few horses we got out there, and shit like that. Sometimes, when we have dope fiends join up, we send them out there to clean out their systems. You know, the good clean country air and all that shit. But it's true. It's nice and clean out there. A man can get his thoughts together."

"Hey, man, someday you got to take us out there," Jackie said excitedly.

Kenyatta looked at him seriously. "I don't mean any disrespect, brothers, 'cause you know I trust you two just as much as I trust anyone in my organization, but we don't allow outsiders on the farm. You have to be in the organization to be able to go out there."

"Bullshit," Billy stated coldly. "You're the fuckin' organization, Kenyatta. You make the rules. If you say we can go, we can go. Ain't nobody to say no except you."

Kenyatta had to grin, even though he didn't want to admit the man's words were true. "Okay, you win that one. If you guys ever need a hiding place, I'll personally put the farm at your disposal."

"Good. That's a whole lot better. When we fuck around with a guy, we like for him to be for real with us, because we are going to be for real with him," Billy replied quickly. "Now let's get down to cases. When can we take this caper off? I see you've been checking it out, so what's the damn holdup now?"

"Only this," Kenyatta said. "Have you guys ever heard about a dope pusher called Little David. I have reason to believe he works for a big pusher or supplier who goes by the name of King Fisher."

Jackie let out a whistle. "Man, you're really talking about a big nigger when you talk about the King Fisher. He's big shit all right. They don't come any bigger, not if they're black anyway."

Kenyatta drummed a pencil against his desktop as he listened. "The nigger is really that big, huh?" His whole body seemed to be tense as he waited for the reply.

"He's bigger than big—he's the man. If he stopped handling stuff in this city, it would damn near dry up," Jackie continued, not noticing his partner trying desperately to catch his eye.

"I wondered why none of my boys would tell me the real about this cat. Maybe that's it. They thought he was too damn big for us to touch."

"Man," Jackie added quickly, not paying heed to Billy's loud moan, "the guy is too big for you or us to go after. He's got some of the best hit men in the world working for him. We are small, small, small potatoes when it comes to him. He don't bullshit, Ken. He'd come down on you so hard, man, you wouldn't know what hit you."

From the glare that came into Kenyatta's eyes,

Jackie should have been warned that his words were only building up Kenyatta's desire to hit the man. The untouchables were the ones he wanted.

"Well," Billy said, trying to change the subject, "we ain't got the time now to worry about no dope dealer no way. We're down to the point where we have to take off this job, 'cause we need money just to eat and sleep."

Kenyatta continued as if he hadn't heard what Billy said. "Now this punk, Little David, he's supposed to work for this guy, King Fisher. He's one of his best pushers, so they tell me. Now, this punk has been warned twice to freeze from pushing junk downtown, but he hasn't paid any heed to it. Twice," Kenyatta said, repeating himself. "We don't warn anybody more than twice. After that, his ass belongs to us."

As he leaned on the desk with his arms under his chin, Billy stared Kenyatta in the eyes for one of the few times in his life. "Maybe you didn't understand me, brother, but I said we ain't got the time to worry about no dope dealer. This is your thing, man. Now, if we weren't pressed for dough like we are, we might have the time to check this out for you, but not now. We are pressed, you understand me, Kenyatta. Pressed, for eatin' and sleepin' cash. If we don't come up with it, we won't even have a pad to call our own."

"Ah yes, I dig where you're coming from, Billy, but it's not as bad as you think." Kenyatta leaned back in his chair and pulled open his desk drawer. He removed a bundle of money that was still in a wrapper. He tossed it on the desk in front of Billy. "Now there's exactly five hundred dollars in that bundle. If by chance you're interested in what I've got for you, it's yours, plus two more bundles the same size as that one. All three of them are yours, if you want the job."

"What job?" Billy asked, not bothering to pick up the bundle. He knew that anything Kenyatta paid for was trouble. If it wasn't, Kenyatta would have sent some of his own men out on the job.

"I want this punk Little David hit—tonight, if it's at all possible," Kenyatta answered, closing his desk drawer.

"What I'd like to know, Kenyatta, is why wouldn't you save yourself some cash by sending your own people out on this job instead of paying us to do it for you," Billy inquired as he picked up the bundle and thumbed through it.

"That's a good question," Kenyatta answered slowly. "Why don't I use my own men is simple. I don't have any people down here at the present time who are professional enough to send out on a job like this. Yes, up on the farm are people who could handle it, but they're busy training some new recruits. Now the few people I do have down here have the nerve but not the experience. You and your friend have both, the nerve and experience. So I'd rather pay you to handle the job. That way I know it's done right."

For the first time Billy glanced over at his partner to see how he was taking it. Jackie shrugged his shoulders, letting Billy know he didn't care one way or the other. It was up to Billy. If he took the job, they would handle it.

"Make it two grand even, Kenyatta, and we'll take care of it for you," Billy replied, as he broke open the pack and split the money down into two even piles. He didn't even wait for Kenyatta's answer before he tossed his partner half the money.

As Kenyatta watched this exchange between the

two men he slowly smiled that cold, calculating smile that never seemed to reach his eyes. If I had a dozen men like these two, he was thinking, I could control the whole city.

"Well then, I take it we have a deal, Billy," he said standing. "Betty, would you and Carol mind running upstairs and fixing my friends a drink. I think we could all use one right about now." He reached down and removed a brown folder from his desk. "I believe you'll find everything you'll need to know in here about Little David, Billy. In fact, it's got everything in it but the time he's going to die, and I think you and Jackie can furnish that little bit of information now."

9

It had been a slow day. Billy and Jackie had sat in the car down on John R and watched Little David take care of all his business. "You know, Jackie, this punk has to be paying off somebody, 'cause the way he sells them drugs I'd swear he had a license. Nobody, and I mean nobody, in their right mind would sell drugs outright like that if they weren't paying off." They watched the man crumble the brown paper bag he had used to carry his drugs in.

One of his bodyguards held a shopping bag that was full of the money the man had taken in. They had stood on the street corner in front of a restaurant and sold every package of dope he had had in the bag. Now the men were preparing to go home. This was the third day Billy and Jackie had watched. They knew where David would go from here. The man had an apartment downtown in one of the most expensive hotels.

Looks like it's going to have to be like you said yesterday, Billy," Jackie stated from the passenger side of the car. "We goin' just have to hit all three of them 'cause you ain't goin' catch him away from his babysitters."

As they sat there, a tall dark-complexioned man walked slowly past the car. They had observed him purchasing drugs from the pusher two days in a row.

"I wonder what's with that motherfucker," Jackie said sharply as he sat up and stared hard at the man. "He seems to take an interest in us that I don't really like."

"Yeah, I noticed him checkin' us out yesterday, Jackie. What you think? Maybe we ought to lean on him a little. That way he won't be so curious about other people next time."

Jackie hesitated, "I hate to bring attention down on us, you know. The less people that notice us the better off we are."

"That bastard can identify us. I wonder who the fuck he is?" Billy stared after the retreating man's back. "There's one thing in our favor, though. We can identify him too. He won't be hard to find. A junkie like him won't change his neighborhood too fast. Maybe we should take care of him first. He knows we've been watching David, so when we make the hit, he's going to put two and two together."

"Before they could make up their minds, the man disappeared in one of the two-story buildings facing the street.

"I don't like this job no kind of way," Jackie stated slowly. "I didn't really care for it when we got it and care less for it now."

"It's kind of late in the day to be speaking against it now, ain't it, partner?" Billy inquired as he started up the motor.

The late-model Cadillac that David used pulled up and he got in with his two bodyguards. The driver of the car hardly slowed down to pick the men up.

"You know," Billy said as he watched the car pull away from the curb, "we could hit them going down the street. David always sits on the side right behind the driver, so we wouldn't have to knock out nobody but him and the driver. That way, we'd make sure no kind of pursuit was behind us."

"You don't think the windows are bulletproof, do you?" Jackie asked.

Billy rubbed his chin. "Naw, they ain't hardly bulletproof. The cat ain't that big, but too much could go wrong. You know how heavy the cops ride this way. It would be our fuckin' luck to make the hit, then run right into a squad car. Naw, man, it wouldn't work; our luck just might be against us." Billy sat behind the wheel, undecided. He removed his cigarettes and lit one. He let his eyes run up and down the street, then slowly examined the other side of it. "I think we should take a little walk," he said and cut the motor.

Jackie got out and stretched his long legs. Then the two men crossed the street; a pair of eyes from the hallway window two buildings down the street followed their every move.

Billy led the way down the alley, then he cut across a backyard until he reached the building he wanted. The back door was open wide, so the men didn't have any problem entering from the rear. Their heels sounded loud in the hallway. When they reached the front of the building, Billy stopped and glanced out; then he led the way upstairs and checked the hallway windows looking out onto the front.

"We can either rent a room on the front or just bulldoze our way in, or we can use the front doorway. Which one would you like, Jackie?"

"I don't give a fuck one way or the other, Billy. Just let me know how the fuck are we supposed to get out of this dump after the hit is made?"

"Now that's the next problem for us to figure out. Which is the quickest way out of this motherfucker after the work is over?" Billy spoke softly as he led the way back down the stairway. He stopped and examined the front door again. "Yeah, Jackie, this might just be the quickest way. Use the doorway here. With both of us on the case, we shouldn't have to worry about somebody coming up on us and taking us by surprise. Naw, if we both look out close, we can handle it right from the hallway."

Jackie just nodded his head in agreement. Whatever Billy came up with, he generally went along with it. "It sounds cool, man. Now if we can only find someplace to put the car, we'll be all right."

They went back out the way they came in. Billy led the way. He checked on the alley. "No, I don't think the alley will work. The cops might see the car parked back here and pull back in the alley to check it out." They walked back towards the car in silence as Billy studied the few escape routes open to them. "We ain't got too many choices, man. If we left one man in the car, then the other one would have to worry about somebody coming down the stairway and blowing the hit."

Jackie snapped his fingers. "Why don't we use Carol, man? She can drive, and she's got all the nerve you could want."

It was a few seconds before Billy would comment on Jackie's suggestion. Then he shook his head. "We ain't never used anybody on a job with us before, man. I don't really like the idea, but if it would stop us from gettin' busted, I'd have to go along with it." The more Billy thought about the matter, the better he liked it. "It might just work out at that, Jackie. I ain't worried about the broad. Kenyatta used her on that hit on the cops, so we know she's damn cool as far as not talking, or he'd never have pulled her along on that job."

"There's that motherfucker again," Jackie said suddenly as the tall, dark man saw them and hurried back into the building. "If you see that motherfucker tomorrow when you're lookin' down that barrel, be sure to put a couple of well-placed slugs in his ass. That motherfucker could cause us a lot of trouble. I don't like having no bastard walking around who can point us out," Jackie stated seriously.

Billy agreed with him wholeheartedly as he started the motor up. "It will be the first time a bastard could put the finger on us, Jackie, but all we have to do is come in the back way so the bastard can't place us tomorrow. We make damn sure he doesn't see us, that's all." Billy wasn't as relaxed about it as he let on. "When we find the time, we'll come back down and pay our nosey friend a little visit. Jackie, if by chance I forget about it, you remind me," Billy said as he pulled away from the curb.

All that night the two men sat up planning their next day's job. They went over it until each knew

actually what he had to do. The car they were to use
would be rented early in the morning under an
assumed name. Next would come the weapons.
Neither man wanted to be arrested with the weapons
in the car. Using Carol would help them out there.
She could drive the second car, carrying the guns in it.

Neither man got much sleep that night. Billy lay
awake staring at the ceiling, while Jackie had Carol
keep him company. He clutched the woman closely
all night, making love to her off and on, until daybreak came streaming through his window. Then and
only then did he finally fall asleep, and both men over-
slept. It was close to twelve o'clock before they got
up. Carol allowed them to sleep late, then she got up
and prepared them a quick breakfast. She woke her
man first, then knocked on Billy's door.

They got up and ate hurriedly, then prepared to
leave, picking up the guns and putting them in the
trunk of the rented car Carol was to drive. One rifle
with a scope on it, plus two thirty-eights, in case they
had to shoot their way out of the building. After that
they were ready. They parked the first car on
Woodward in front of the Holiday Inn on the street.
If everything went right, they'd transfer over to this
car and leave the one they were riding in. Then they
climbed into the car with Carol and she drove slowly toward their destination. In a matter of minutes they
were there.

Undecided on whether or not she should turn up in
the alley, Carol slowed down, but Billy spoke up.
"Keep on going, honey. We're going to get out on that
side street and cut through some yards." He glanced
down at his watch. "Everybody check their watches,"
he ordered, remembering how Kenyatta had done it.

"Carol, at exactly five minutes after one you pull into the alley. Make sure it's exactly five minutes after one, because we'll be coming out of there at just that time. I'm going to leave the rifle behind, so that we won't draw any attention that we don't want."

Well, looks like this is about it," Jackie said as Carol pulled up and parked where she was directed to. Both men got out and glanced up and down the street as Carol opened the trunk. The rifle was long, but it was in a wrapper. They stuck the pistols inside their pants, then hurried towards the nearest yard.

They made their way through the yards, coming out in the rear of the house that they wanted. No one had really paid any attention to them.

Just as on the day before, Billy led the way toward the front of the building. It was deserted except for an alley cat that ran at the sight of the two men. Billy glanced out of the broken window in the front doorway. As he observed the street, Jackie checked the hallway. If anyone was to come along while the men were getting ready to make their hit, Jackie was to hold them at gunpoint until after Billy cut down the dope pusher. Then and only then, Jackie was to cut the witness down with his pistol.

"So far so good," Jackie murmured.

"Here comes our boy," Billy stated, keeping Jackie up on what was happening out on the street. "Just like we hoped, the bastard continues to use the same routine day after day. He must not be able to sell the drugs from inside the poolroom or restaurant, so he has to use that doorway over there. He's standing out on the sidewalk now, prancing for the women."

David considered himself quite a ladies' man. While one of his lieutenants stood in the nearest door-

way taking care of the customers that came along,
David stood out on the sidewalk collecting the money.
After an addict paid him, he would tell the bodyguard
nearest him what the man was buying. This man
would relay the price of the buy to the man in the
doorway, who would then give the addict what he paid
for. If a bust ever went down, the only man who could
really end up with a case was the one in the doorway,
because he was the only one with drugs in his possession. Only if funny money was used could David
end up with a case. But he had a fighting chance,
because the addicts never got the drugs directly from
him.

Billy took his time and removed the rifle from the
cover. He checked out the scope, then took deliberate
aim, zeroing in on David's small chest. The sound of
the rifle going off in the hallway was loud, almost
busting the eardrums of the two men. As David was
thrown back by the strong blow, Billy took aim and
hit him again. He searched the street quickly for the
drug addict they wanted, but the man was nowhere in
sight. He didn't have to wipe the gun off because he
had used a pair of light rubber gloves. He just dropped
the rifle and started swiftly down the hall. Jackie was
right at his heels.

A man started to open his door to glance out and
Jackie snapped off a quick shot at the man's head. At
the sound of the gunshot, other doors that had started to open quickly closed. The two men made their
way out of the building without anyone really getting
a good look at them. Billy glanced at his watch as
they made their way through the yard. He realized at
once that he had made the kill too quickly. Now they
would have to wait at least one minute for their ride.

"We're going to be early, Jackie. I should have held up and then this shit would have gone off like clockwork."

Jackie gave his frequently used shrug, which meant he didn't give a shit one way or the other. When they reached their destination, the car hadn't arrived. The men stepped back out of sight in a gangway and waited. Carol arrived thirty seconds later, to both men's joy. They rushed out and jumped in the car before it had even stopped. Then they ducked down so that it looked as if she was alone.

Carol drove slowly through the alley. When she reached Brush Street she pulled out into the oncoming traffic slowly, making sure she didn't break any laws. Suddenly, as she moved down the street with the traffic, a police car pulled up beside her. She smiled politely at the black officer on the passenger side. The officer smiled back, flirting with her. Then the driver of the police car put on his lights and they took off, with the siren screaming.

"Looks like we're just about home free," she said, as she turned off and headed for their other car.

10

On the outskirts of town in the penthouse of a swank apartment building the phone rang softly. A man in a dark business suit picked up the receiver and spoke into it for a few seconds, then he hung up. He made his way to the rear of the penthouse, where the inside swimming pool was located.

"King Fisher," he called out in a low voice, "somebody just knocked off that little punk David."

"Who the hell is David?" a tall, tan-complexioned black man asked. His voice had a mellow sound to it, yet it was firm. One could tell he was used to giving orders.

"You know," the man said again, trying not to speak

115

too loudly, "Little David, the kid that handles that east-side action downtown. You got it together now, boss?"

The King Fisher waved his hand at the beautiful woman lying on the rug next to him. "Go fix yourself a drink, Vickie. Take a long time while you're at it."

He waited until the white girl in the bikini disappeared before he spoke again. The swinging of her well-shaped hips was enough to hold any man's attention, but with the walk she had, it drew them like flies. "Pretty good-lookin' stuff, huh?" King Fisher asked.

"You always pick the best, boss," the man answered truthfully. "I just wish I had your taste."

"Taste hell. Money, you mean, don't you, Sam?" King Fisher inquired sharply. "Now, what's this shit about Little David getting hit?"

"That's it, boss. Somebody took a rifle and knocked him out of the box from across the street. He was on our corner gettin' rid of the dope when he was hit. There was no attempt to rob him or nothing, just a straight-out hit."

King Fisher stood up. He was tall, at least two inches over six feet. His hair was graying around the edges, still wavy from the last process he had gotten. His dark eyes glittered dangerously as he started to pace up and down alongside his pool.

"So the kid was right after all," King Fisher stated after a minute. "You know he called and told me he had been warned about selling drugs in the city. Seems as if some fuckin' organization is out to close down all pushers. I told him don't worry about it, I'd handle it from here. So now he's dead, and ain't nothing been done."

King Fisher stopped his pacing. "Who the hell did I put on the job of checking this shit out?" He glared at Sam. "Do you remember anything about this shit, Sam? Didn't I say I was going to send somebody downtown to check this shit out?"

"Yeah, boss, you were going to send somebody, then I think it slipped your mind, 'cause you didn't say anything else about it."

"You should have reminded me about it, Sam. What's wrong, man? You falling down on the job?" King Fisher glared at his bodyguard. He had to blame somebody for it, though he knew he was totally responsible for what had happened. He hadn't taken care of his business. "It's something Little David told me too," King Fisher continued. "The kid said the warning was for me also, and I only laughed about it." The King Fisher fell silent then as he realized that he could have been knocked out of the box just like David had been. Neither one of them had taken the warning to heart, and now David was dead.

"Sam, I want you to put some of our best men on this. Let the word out that I'm giving up five grand for word on who made this hit, then we'll see. Yeah, we'll get to the bottom of this shit, and quick!"

"Okay, boss," Sam answered, glad that the big man had forgotten to hold Sam responsible for not reminding him about the trouble. Things like that could get a guy killed, Sam reflected as he waited for the rest of his orders. Now all he wanted to do was get out of the King Fisher's sight for a while, because it was a bad place to be when the King Fisher was aroused.

"Have Vickie bring me out a drink when she comes back, Sam, and also tell the boys to double-check anybody who tries to come in to see me. We had better make sure everybody is checked out real close, and man, I want you to personally see to it that my orders are carried out. No more mistakes, Sam. You dig where I'm coming from? I don't like to take chances on my life, and it looks like we just took a big one."

"Okay, King, I'll handle everything, just like you want it done," Sam answered, starting to back out.

"Oh, Sam, get in touch with Little David's boys and put one of his closest men in charge. Use one that knows just how the operation goes. We'll continue to supply them with stuff, but make sure you pick a winner, man. Don't come up with no punk who might end up one day turning state's evidence against us," King Fisher ordered, waving his hand to add emphasis to his order. The huge diamond on his finger glittered wildly as his hand went back and forth. "Also be sure to find out the name of this organization that's trying to put the pushers out of business. I want this tonight, Sam. Tonight, do you understand?"

Sam understood too well. He almost broke and ran from the room. He had a lot to do, and he would have to put pressure on those under him. When the boss got scared, there was no telling what he might do, and the boss was scared now. Anytime someone got knocked off in their organization, the boss got shook. For a heavyset man, Sam moved swiftly. He weighed over two hundred pounds. He was an ex-boxer and policeman. He had gotten caught taking bribes and was kicked off the force, but since then he'd made more money than he'd ever dreamed of. So he hadn't really lost anything except a steady job that took up too much of his time.

Working for the King Fisher was a sweet job, except for times like this. Well, it wouldn't last.

Whoever the upstart was would be quickly taken care of. Sam would personally see to that. His very existence depended on it.

Meanwhile, back in the ghetto, Kenyatta had just heard the news by phone. He broke out some expensive wine and was drinking it when his two hit men came through the door.

"Hey, what you goin' say," he yelled out in greeting. "You know, Billy, you boys are better than I realized. You don't waste any time, do you?" He smiled at the men, then called out to Betty. "Honey, find some more glasses so that we can get our brothers here relaxed. I know they'd love to have a glass of this good wine."

Billy flopped down in his chair. "Yeah, I could use some, if it's cold," he said as he straightened out his legs. The butterflies inside his stomach were just beginning to leave. It took awhile after a job for him to relax.

"How did everything go?" Kenyatta inquired as the men made themselves comfortable.

"Just like clockwork," Jackie said, popping his fingers. "I mean, you couldn't ask for a better job. It was pure sweetness."

"Uh huh," Kenyatta mumbled as he pulled his desk drawer open. He removed the packs of money and tossed them on the desk. "I think these belong to you boys," he said, leaning back in his chair. He watched Jackie pick up the money. The man took the three bundles, tossed one to Billy, stuck one in his pocket, and tossed the other one over to Carol.

"We didn't talk about it, Billy, but I feel as if she earned one, man," he said, shaking his head as she attempted to give the bundle back. "Keep it, baby. If

I didn't want you to have it, woman, I wouldn't have given it to you."

Billy laughed loudly. "He's right, Carol. You really earned it, girl. When I saw that car pull up in the alley, I would have gladly given you all three of the bundles just for that lift!"

"You can say that again," Jackie added. "My ass was shaking like a dog eating pumpkin seeds and shittin' turds!"

"It wasn't all that bad. You guys just said it went like a dream, didn't you?" Kenyatta asked, curious.

"We were a minute off in our timing," Billy explained shortly. "We got there a minute before our ride was supposed to arrive. You know that timing shit is the key to everything, man. If your timing is off, you can blow the whole fuckin' caper."

Kenyatta shook his head in agreement. Timing was one of the points he was trying to drill into his military men up at the farm. It was all important. Without it, you might as well hope for blind luck. "Now that you boys have got that over with, I guess you'll want to take a rest before knockin' off the food-stamp joint, huh?"

"Not hardly, man. We need the bread. This little shit we made from you ain't about nothin', man. We use it for fuck-around money. Naw, we're still ready to knock off that joint, Kenyatta, whenever you make up your mind to go for it."

"It's gratifying as hell to run into some guys so dedicated," Kenyatta replied as he studied the men. "But all work and no play is bad for your health, man, so I'm going to give a little party for you guys. After that, we'll get down to business, okay?"

"What the hell," Billy answered. "Why not. We

might as well enjoy ourselves. Money ain't shit if you can't find the time to have fun with it."

"That's the spirit, Billy," Kenyatta said. "Let's let our hair down for a minute, anyway. Suppose I set it up for tonight? That way we can have big fun and not waste too much time."

The men laughed together. It was a relaxing time. They had taken off a hard job, and now it was time to enjoy themselves.

When Betty returned with the drinks and Kenyatta told her about the party, she smiled brightly. "Hey, daddy, that should be real hip. We ain't really swung around here in quite a while." The sound of her voice was like bells tinkling.

Billy couldn't help but stare at her. "I sure hope there's another girl in your organization like Betty, man. If so, I might even join up."

Kenyatta started to say something hip in return, but he saw the hunger in the man's eyes and knew that he was looking at a lonely person. "I'm sure you'll be able to find somebody who will knock you to your knees, Billy." He hesitated, then said, "Betty, you know what? I was thinking about calling the guys and girls out at the farm. Tell them I said to start a barbecue and to put some beer and wine on ice. We're on our way."

He glanced over to the men. "We can have more fun out there than we'll ever have here. Let's gas up and head for the country. I'll bet it will be something you two will never forget."

It was a small convoy that drove out of town. There were six carloads of men and women traveling to enjoy the party. Billy and Jackie rode alone with Carol. She sat in the middle while Billy did the driving. Kenyatta was driving the lead car with Betty, and another couple made use of the backseat.

They hadn't been driving over an hour before Kenyatta pulled off the freeway and headed down a two-way highway. The houses began to get farther and farther apart, until nothing more than an occasional farmhouse could be seen. Kenyatta turned off the paved road and led them down a dirt one. The dust coming off his tires was so heavy that at times Billy could hardly see ahead. Finally the lead car turned into a pathway that led up to a large white farmhouse. As the men gazed out the windows they could see people coming out of the six smaller houses that surrounded the large, white-frame one. People were everywhere, smiling and waving as they drove up.

"Those little houses are for the married couples," Carol informed them.

"Hey, baby, are my eyes playing tricks on me or are those really cows I see back there behind the buildings," Jackie asked curiously.

"Yeah, honey, they're cows, and we've also got some pigs and chickens on the place," Carol answered with a note of pride in her voice.

"We!" Billy remarked with sarcasm. "You mean to say you believe Kenyatta will share this shit with the rest of ya?"

"You don't have to believe it if you don't want to, Billy, but everything on this place belongs to everybody in the organization. Anyone who wants to can move out here and live, rent free. Where else can a black person stay, rent free, food free, and everything else free? When they eat pig, you eat pig. That's why I say it's ours. If I want to, I can move out here for the rest of my life. No more worry about rent and the rest of that shit that bugs the ordinary person in the city."

"It sounds good, honey. Now all you got to do is talk Jackie into joining up and moving out here with you, and you can relax for the rest of your life."

"Funny, funny, funny. You know, Billy, I never realized in all this time that you're a real funny guy," Jackie said with no humor in his voice.

"Now, don't you two start fussing. It ain't nothing

wrong with what he said, Jackie. If you and I were to move out here, what would be so bad about it?" She glanced over at him, her eyes large and shining.

"Well, honey, when you put it like that, I can't see anything wrong with it," Jackie replied.

Billy smiled encouragingly as they got out of the car. "Find me a girl like Betty, Carol, and I'd gladly move out here with her." It might have been said in a joking manner, but she could read the seriousness in his voice.

He's really got a case on Betty, she thought silently, as she took both men's arms and led them up the path towards the house. People were waving and calling out to her as they got closer and closer to the farmhouse, until she had to release them so she could wave at friends.

"Everybody does look healthy and happy," Jackie stated as he examined the faces they passed. "I mean, these guys and gals really look like they dig this country life.

"Why do you think so many of our members are out here on the farm instead of back in the city at our club?" she asked seriously.

"I thought they were out here going through some kind of training," Billy replied.

"Some of them are, but most of them are finished with that jive, and they'd rather stay out here than back there. You just have to stay out here to understand it, man. You don't have no police harrassment, and for a black man that is something in itself. A man can completely forget the color of his skin out here. It don't make no difference if you're black or green. Don't nobody bother you about it. Whereas, back in the city, a black man is constantly on his guard because of the white pigs fuckin' with him."

"Hey, young lady, that's strong language for one so tiny," Jackie warned her, holding her arm tightly.

She smiled up at him. "Okay, sweet man, I'm warned. I won't forget I'm a lady again, okay?"

He grinned. "That's something you could never forget, honey, that you're a lady. It's all over you, There's nothing you can do about it."

Carol stopped and introduced them to some people, then led them towards the rear of the house, where the wonderful smells were coming from. In the back there was an open barbecue pit with ribs piled high on it. Next to it were smaller pits with chickens and steaks cooking; an open tub was filled with beer cans and unopened bottles of wine.

"It's not every day that they have a party out here, so they're going to really let their hair down," Carol warned as she took them by the arm and steered them towards the house.

"Tell me something, Carol. Ain't all the girls spoken for out here?" Billy asked.

"No way," she answered quickly. "You see that little house over there?" she said and pointed her finger to show where she was talking about. "Well, that's where the single girls stay until they find a man they like and choose him. You'd be surprised just how many free ladies there are out here. I'd say at least five or six anyway."

"Five or six, huh? Well, that ain't too many," Billy replied seriously.

"Well, how many do you need. I'd think one would be enough if you could find the right one," Carol stated, getting angry with him but not wanting to show it.

She opened the back door and shoved them through.
In the kitchen two women were busy handling pots
and pans. "Hi, Jean, Connie," she called out. She
quickly introduced her two escorts to the women, then
continued on.

Billy glanced back at the cute brown-skinned girl
called Connie. "Hey, man, I really like what I seen
just then," he stated.

Carol just grinned and continued to lead them
through the house. She took them upstairs and showed
them the bedrooms. "You have to stay out here quite
awhile before you can get one of those," she said.
"These generally go to the people who work on the
place and aren't going back to the city for quite a
while. There's a long list of people waiting for them."

When they came back downstairs Betty had a tall
dark-complexioned woman with her. She hurried over
to them. "Hey, I got somebody for you to meet! This
is Joy. Joy, the short one is Billy, and that tall guy
happens to be Carol's love of life. His name is Jackie."

She stayed with them for a few minutes, then
departed. Joy took Billy's arm and they started walking around the farm. It was late evening before they
ran into Kenyatta.

With him was a tall dark man whose head was as
clean-shaven as Kenyatta's. As the two men stood in
the firelight of the bonfires, they looked to be brothers. But as one got near them, it was obvious that the
clean-shaven heads were the only thing the men had
in common. Both men were tall but, where Kenyatta
had a heavy beard, Ali, the brother next to him, had
none. Both men had heavy black mustaches, yet there
was a difference even in those. Ali's mustache came
down in the style of Fu Manchu.

Kenyatta noticed them near one of the large bonfires that had been made in the backyard. He came
over with his companion. "Hi, brothers, I hope you've
been havin' a good time," he inquired in the way of
a greeting, then continued. "This big bastard next to
me is Ali. I guess you could call him my right-hand
man. He runs the farm for me, or the club in the city
whenever I'm out here. We generally switch around.
One of us is always at one place or the other."

The men quickly shook hands, then Kenyatta
noticed the woman with Billy. "I see you've found
the finest black woman on the farm, Miss Joy. She's
really something else, Billy," Kenyatta said as he
reached out and pulled the woman over to him. He
gave her a big bear hug. "This is Betty's aunt, Billy,
believe it or not. You can damn near tell from lookin'
at them. They do resemble each other a little, but my
woman is finer!"

"I have to say that's a matter of opinion," Billy
replied truthfully, as he grabbed her arm and pulled
her back towards his side of the fire. Joy did resemble Betty slightly, but she was bigger. Her nose was
longer, lips wider, hips bigger, yet both women had
the same walk. Billy had been overwhelmed by her
since they had met, and now he was even more drawn
to the woman. She was his kind of woman. He liked
them tall and black. And after talking to her he knew
she was intelligent.

For some reason Joy was drawn to the short, husky
man. His seriousness was not the only factor that
attracted her. She knew he liked her, and not for just
the thought of going to bed with her either. She could
tell the man was lonely yet very choosy. He carried
himself like a man, even in front of Kenyatta, where

she had seen a lot of men give up their manhood unknowingly, going out of their way to be accepted by Kenyatta. That was one of the main reasons she hadn't chosen a man yet. Most of the ones she came in contact with out on the farm were followers, men who had to look up to another man to tell them what to do. She couldn't stand a man who didn't believe he was a leader. At once she recognized this quality in Billy. He wasn't a follower. He led. She could tell that, from the way Billy and Jackie got along, Billy was actually the leader. He didn't flaunt his leadership; it just came to him.

She wrapped her arm around his. "Ken, you should have brought this man out here long ago. We're in dire need of men like him," she stated in a husky voice.

The group of men laughed. "Maybe I should have. Anyway, honey, I'm giving this small party for him and his partner, so maybe that will make up for my neglect."

"I hope the sheriff don't come out," Jackie said as he stared around at the huge fires burning. "Seems to me one of your neighbors just might call them, seeing all these fires going."

Kenyatta glanced at the bonfires. "If they should show up, we can handle it. But as far as neighbors, we don't have one closer than five miles. They leave us alone, and we do the same."

"How long are we going to stay up here?" Billy inquired.

"Why? Don't tell me you're in a hurry to get back to the city?"

"Naw, brother, that's why I'm asking. I ain't in no hurry," Billy said seriously. He pinched Joy's arm and smiled at her. "I could stay up here for the next year now."

Kenyatta laughed loudly. "Yeah, man, I think I understand right where you're coming from. But to answer your question, this party won't last but a day or two. Whenever we have one, it's generally over sometime the next day. So if you're tired by then, we'll be going back."

Ali spoke up for the first time. "I've had the cabin over there on your right fixed up for you guys. There's two bedrooms inside, plus a shower, so you'll have as much privacy as you could want."

"Good," Jackie said quickly. "I was wondering if we'd have to sleep in the car. Because of my height, the idea of sleepin' in a ride tonight didn't appeal to me."

The way he said it made the small group of people laugh together. There was a feeling of warmth between them. It seemed to spread until everybody on the farm felt it. A feeling of brotherhood, black love, love for each other.

As the night passed slowly, couples began to slip off into the darkness. The music coming from the house began to change. Instead of the hot, driving beat of soul that made you want to dance, it now became soft, lovers' music.

Billy sat under a tree, nursing a drink, while holding Joy in his arms. He could feel the woman's heartbeat as he turned her towards him and kissed her slowly. "Joy, I don't know how to say it, honey, but I wish I had come out here sooner and met you. It's as if a new world has opened for me. It's hard to believe that you don't have anybody."

She smiled in the darkness. Not used to jumping to

conclusions, she hated to make a choice so soon but still realized that it would have to be a quick decision. "Billy, I don't even know how to begin. I can't say I'm in love, but I can tell you I'm damn interested in you. But what kind of woman would you take me for if I gave myself to you tonight? I don't want you to think I'm some sort of tramp, honey."

For an answer Billy kissed her lips until they were sealed. "That's your answer, honey. How could I think anything about you except happiness. That's what you bring to me. Pure happiness." Again he kissed her slowly. Their kisses were not wild but full of tender passion.

"Honey," she began, "it's really too soon. How can either of us be sure? I mean, we just met, yet I feel as if we've known each other for years." She removed her arms from around his neck. "Billy, I just don't want to be hurt again. The last man I loved tried to take advantage of me. When he found out I really cared, he wanted to make a whore out of me. It's not that I wouldn't work for my man, it's just that I don't believe a man could really love me if he wanted me to work the streets for him."

"Darling," Billy began, the word sounding strange to his ears, "something like that you don't even have to worry about. Joy, I'm a man, and I think I get enough money for me and my woman. I know it's too soon to be talkin' about you being my lady, but give it some thought, hear?"

For an answer, Joy stood up and took his hand. She led the way across the farmyard towards the small white cabin sitting back in the dark. The door didn't take a key. It opened when she twisted the doorknob. Inside, the cabin was dark and Joy felt around until she found the light switch. The small bulb lit the room dimly. Joy didn't stop in the small cabin's tiny front room, which was used for a kitchen also. There were three other doors leading from the front.

"That door on your right, Billy, is the bathroom. The other door leads to the bedroom that Carol and Jackie will use. This is our room, honey," she stated in a deep voice as she pushed open the door. The bed in the room was a simple wooden one, with a large mattress on it.

Joy didn't waste any time after entering the room. She quickly slipped out of the blue jeans she had been wearing. Billy watched her out of the corner of his eyes. When she came out of the shirt she had on, he knew he had been right. He had sworn to himself all day that she didn't have a bra on; now he knew he had been correct. He quickly took his clothes off.

As he undressed, Joy pulled back the covers and jumped in the bed. "You may not believe it, honey, but you're the first man I've had in six months. I came out here about four months ago. Before that, I'd left my man and kept an apartment in the city on the west side with another girl." She stopped for breath, then added, "So, Billy, you can say you're gettin' a six-month-old cherry." Her laughter followed, low and deep, the sound of a happy woman.

As Billy neared the bed, she opened her arms and stretched towards him. She gave him the feeling of being wanted. He came to her then, taking his time as he let himself down beside her. They embraced, kissing tenderly at first, then from the heat of their love, more violently as their passions became aroused.

A low moan escaped from Billy as an enveloping awareness overcame him. His masculinity became swollen, larger than he believed possible. It had never gotten that big. He could feel it vibrating between his legs like a plucked string, constant in its movements.

When Joy's hand came under the sheet searching for his manhood, it came in contact with the steadily increasing rod. Her happy gasp of joy filled him with a joyous warmth. Billy clutched her to him tightly. It was all he could do to stop from having premature climax. His hands fumbled under the sheet, feeling only the softness of her skm. She ain't got nothing on! The words exploded in his mind. He felt the hairs on her body, which only aroused him more.

"Come on, honey," she moaned in his ear. "Take me, Billy, take me!" It was more like an order than anything else. He wanted to take her but tried to hold back. He didn't want to come too soon. Her legs spread open and he found himself on top of her yet not remembering ever having climbed on top of her. The first time didn't last thirty seconds. He could feel himself coming. Joy never allowed him to stop. He came, screaming out silently against her neck. She pushed up against him, forcing him to stay in her. Her hips moved, grinding and twisting until he could feel himself growing again.

The second time was more controlled. This time, Billy knew what he was doing. He moved on top of her with practiced movements. From past experience he knew how to please her. His movements matched hers. When she moaned with pleasure, he clutched her tighter. His hands pulled her soft, firm ass even closer, until she screamed out loud in her pleasure.

For a time they seemed to be struggling against each other. Both of them from their prone positions hunched each other with such force that it seemed as

if someone would be hurt. Her screams became louder until Billy was sure everyone on the farm could
hear them.

"Goddamn, daddy, don't stop now," she cried out
as she felt him beginning to come. He couldn't help
himself. It was there, and no matter how he tried he
couldn't stop the nut from cracking. In his final plunge
he managed to reach that certain spot that set her off.
Joy tightened her grip on his wide shoulders and rode
it out. This was the first time in her life any man had
made her reach four climaxes. They began, one after
the other, until she was weak.

Billy remained on top of her, too weak to move.
For a minute he was like a dead man. The exhilaration was gone; all he could do was merely exist. Too
weak to move, he remained on top of her as pleasant
lethargy overcame him.

The couple remained locked together until they
heard a noise coming from the living room. "That
must be Carol and her fellow," Joy said as she shoved
Billy off. "Honey, you can't make a home up there.
I'm big but not that large," she added, then kissed him
on the cheek as he rolled over.

It was daybreak before Billy drifted off to sleep.
Later on that afternoon, Kenyatta knocked on the door
and entered when Billy called out to him, thinking it
was Jackie.

"What is this?" Kenyatta yelled out as he came
strolling in. "What's the deal here? You people plan
on staying in bed all day?"

Joy snatched the covers over them quickly but not
quite quickly enough. "Damn, that was a pretty good
peep I got, but don't worry, Joy, I've seen tits before.
Maybe not quite as large as yours, girl, but enough

not to get excited over them."

"What brings you out so early?" Billy inquired, trying not to show his irritation. It was foolish of him, he realized, to be angry over Kenyatta's sudden appearance. But he was enjoying himself so much with Joy that he would have disliked anyone's company right at that moment.

"Don't worry, my man, this won't take but a few minutes, then you can get back to wherever you were before I came barging in," Kenyatta replied. He walked over to the nightstand and picked up the half empty cigarette pack. "I'm glad to see someone smokes my brand," he stated as he removed a cigarette from the pack. "Now, let's get down to the real deal. I'm gettin' ready to head back for town, Billy, so I wanted to check with you guys before I left." He waited to see if Billy had anything to say, then continued. "You're welcome to stay out here as long as you like. I'll check back with you by phone about that thing we were talking about." He hesitated, then added, "I was thinkin' the first of the month would be about the best time, Billy. It seems as if they'd have more bread around then, do you agree?"

"Yeah, man, it seems as if that would be the coolish time to me," Billy answered without too much interest.

Kenyatta's eyelids went up. "Hey, my man, what's this shit? You sound as if you don't dig it now. Have you had a change of mind or something?"

"Naw, nothing like that, Kenyatta. I just don't have my mind on it, that's all," Billy said and smiled. "Don't worry, brother, I'll get it together. I just had such a wonderful time out here at your place, man, that it seems like I hate to spoil it by worrying about that other shit back in the city." He hesitated, then added, "I can easily see why some of the brothers come out here and don't want to go back. It's too easy to relax out here, away from all the hustle and bustle that goes on back there. Yeah, you can really relax out here."

Kenyatta laughed loudly. "Shit, Billy, everything gets tiresome, man. Give you a couple of weeks here and you'll be begging to get back to the city."

"Maybe. You just might be right, but I don't really think so," Billy answered him slowly, taking his time and thinking the matter over. "But anyway, I've got to take care of that little matter you were talking about. You say the first. Okay then, fix it up for that day."

"Beautiful," Kenyatta replied. "I'll handle it. You guys goin' lay out here until then, or what?"

"Maybe, just maybe. I hadn't given it any thought, Ken, but after talking to Jackie I'll know. Any way it goes, we have our own car, so it won't be no problem for us to get back to the city."

Joy spoke up suddenly, "I've got to go into the city sometime this week, honey, and see my little boy."

Kenyatta smiled down at the couple. "Well, it looks like you're going to be coming in sooner than you realized after all, huh?" He laughed abruptly.

"Fuck you, Kenyatta," Billy said good-naturedly. "I don't know what I'm going to do. I just woke up and here you were, so I'm not sure of anything. Give me time, man. At least time to wake up good. Who knows, Jackie might even want to go back today."

"Okay, then," Kenyatta said, "just be sure to get in touch with me, that's all. I want to be able to reach you if something should come up, so just keep in touch." He stopped at the doorway. "By the way, Billy, I just want you to know, man, that Ali's in charge out here, so if you should have any problems or questions about something, just run him down and he'll be able to put your boots on for you. Oh yeah, if by chance you should want to get in touch with me, as long as it's important, he'll also know where I can be reached, other than at the club."

Billy sat up in the bed. "Hey, Kenyatta, I been meaning to ask, man, how can I find you if you ain't at the club? You want to give me another address or phone number or something?"

Kenyatta grinned. "Not yet, baby, not yet," he said and went out the door. The couple in the bed could hear him joking with Jackie, then silence. They didn't waste any more time. They both turned at the same time, so that Joy was quickly held in a firm grip. Her arms went around his neck, embracing him tightly.

12

In the late afternoon, as Kenyatta and some of his group drove swiftly back towards town, Detective Benson and his partner sat in their office pondering the latest killing to be dropped on their laps. The other detectives in homicide had just walked out from a briefing where the chief of police had read the riot act to them: either make some arrests on some of the latest murders or get ready to see certain changes made in the personnel.

Some changes would be made, and none of them wanted to be the officers shifted around. It would look bad on the record, plus it would be a cut in pay.

"It seemed to me that bastard was looking right at

me," Ryan said for the tenth time.

"I know, I had the same goddamn feeling," Benson admitted. "It seems as if somebody is going to catch hell if something doesn't break around here."

"I had hopes that by now, Ben, some kind of break would have come our way, but there's been nothing. It's as if nobody knows a fuckin' thing about this shit, and I'm sure as hell that the same people are responsible for all these murders."

Benson stared moodily at the ceiling. "I'd have thought that after talkin' to what seems like every goddamn junkie in the city we would have turned up something. But no, not one damn break!"

"Yeah, I know what you mean. We must have talked to over a hundred of the bastards, yet not one of them could give us the information we really needed," Ryan stated, going over in his mind the long hours they had put in talking with various drug addicts.

"We can feel proud of the fact that we've helped narco bust at least ten different pushers," Benson stated. "Them guys in narco have got it made, man. Just kick a few doors down and they got all they need to make their boss happy."

The sudden ringing of the phone made both men alert. Ryan snatched the receiver off the hook. "Don't be in too much of a hurry, man. It might be another killing," Benson said.

"Yeah, yeah, I remember you. James Brown. I been wondering when you'd call. I've been giving you a lot of thought, thinkin' you shitted us to get out that day," Ryan stated, leaning back in his chair. "You're right around the corner, huh. Well come on up. One of us will be waiting downstairs for you, Brown, so hurry up!" Ryan hung the phone up and smiled over at his partner.

"And as for you, Detective Benson," he said, grinning at his partner, "I don't ever want to hear you call these guys human riffraff any more. Come on, I'll explain it to you on the way downstairs. I think our break has come."

Ryan almost ran towards the elevator. "Our boy Brown just might have something for us. He thinks he can pick out the mug shots of the men who put the finishing touches on our pusher man, Little David. Yes sirree, he says he's sure of it. If the boys are in the mug books, we got our break!"

"Did he see them do it?" Benson asked as the elevator arrived.

"No, I don't think he's an eyewitness, or else he doesn't want to get that involved in it. But he says we should appreciate what he's got for us." Before Benson could say anything, he continued. "Appreciate it enough to give him twenty bucks."

"Aw shit," Benson cried, not concealing the disappointment he felt.

Before he could complain, Ryan leaped down his throat. "Just what in the hell are you thinking about, Ben? Here you are crying about the only fuckin' break we've had. Goddamn it, man, I want to break this shit wide open too, but I don't expect the killers to come walking into our office and confess. Nor do I expect an eyewitness to come walking in. Now here we've got a guy who says he can help us, and you're disgusted because the guy's not an eyewitness."

The elevator stopped on the second floor and two uniformed policemen got on. The two men discontinued their conversation at the sight of the two detectives.

"Hey, Ryan, I'm sorry about that. You're one hun-

dred percent right, too. I don't know; it's this fuckin'
steady flow of murders that's gettin' me down. Maybe
I'm not thinking right, or I'm thinking too much about
the case. How many officers have been knocked off
in six months? How many arrests with convictions
have we come up with?" Benson didn't wait for an
answer, he continued. "So I'm guilty of hoping for
too much. I don't know, but I do know you're right
about what you just said."

The elevator came to a halt on the ground floor.
Ryan put his arm around Benson's shoulder. "No, I'm
not right. I'm wrong as hell for jumping on you like
that," he said as they walked away from the staring
officers. "I should know better than anyone how a
man can hope too much. I know exactly why you feel
disappointed. It's because you're such a damn good
cop, that's why."

Before the men could continue their conversation,
the man they were looking for came running up.

James Brown glanced around nervously. "I don't
like to be seen down here," he said in the way of a
greeting.

"Come on then," Ryan said and led him back towards the elevator. Brown didn't say another word until
they were on their way up in the elevator. "Now, what's
this crap about you're pretty sure these boys made the
hit, even though you didn't see them do it?" Ryan
inquired as they reached the third floor and got out.

"It's like this," Brown began. "These two guys were
watching Little David for the past week. I mean, really laying on the guy's tail. That's the reason why I
noticed them. They didn't show up until David did
and didn't leave until after he did. At first I thought
they might be cops, you know, but after gettin' a good

look at them I knew they were hoods. Next, I put them down as a couple of stickup men who were trying to figure out a way to knock off Little David. When I say 'knock off,' I don't mean put him on ice. I just figured they wanted to rip off some of the dope money David was racking up."

Benson led them to the rear of a large office. There was a long counter in the front where two police-women worked, but they went past the counter. He opened a door into a small room with nothing but a desk in it. There were four hard-backed chairs scat-tered about. Benson held the door open for the other two men to enter, then he went back out. In a few minutes he returned, carrying three large books.

"I figured we'd start with the books that contained all our holdup men," he stated as he dropped them on the desk. "Damn, Ryan, you know those bastards are heavy. I don't know how those women handle them!"

"I do," Ryan replied. "They don't try to carry three of them at a time!" Both men laughed, then fell silent as Brown started turning the pages.

He finished the first book quickly. "I saw quite a few people in that one that I know," he said before opening up the second one. He hesitated, then asked, "If I find what I'm lookin' for, you guys are going to kick out the twenty dollars, ain't you?"

The two detectives glanced at each other before one of them made a reply. "You know, we don't make it a habit of kickin' out money. It has to come out of our own pockets, Brown."

Brown shrugged and closed the book. His inten-tions were plain. "Man, that's why I asked you about the twenty before I came up. I didn't want any mis-understanding."

"You wouldn't like to try out the ninth-floor lock-up, would you?" Benson inquired harshly. His temper was at the boiling point. It wouldn't take much to make him slap the man in front of him.

Brown shook his head. "Naw, man, I don't want to get locked up, but that wouldn't help you bust this case open either."

"Okay, Brown. You find the picture, then we'll see what we can do about your twenty," Ryan said, playing the part of the peacemaker.

Reluctantly, Brown began to thumb through the mug shots again. He worked his way through the book slowly until he was almost finished with it. Then he saw what he wanted and stopped. Under their pictures were the nicknames, "Mutt" and "Jeff." Quickly Brown glanced at the address: *no known address.* He quickly memorized all the information he could. This was what he had come for, this very information, not for the funky twenty-dollar bill he was trying to milk out of the officers. The cheap bastards, he called them under his breath. Brown was shooting for way more than chump change. He had heard the wire on the streets; the information in front of him was worth far more than twenty dollars. Yes sirree, he told himself, the King Fisher would pay big stuff for this little bit of shit. He debated whether or not to tell the police anything, then decided it might be best to be honest with them. He might need a favor one day.

"These two cats here," he said and pointed his finger at them. "I couldn't forget them two guys no kind of way. This one motherfucker looks as if he ought to be playing basketball with the Globetrotters or somebody. Maybe even the Pistons, you know what I mean? The cat is really tall."

Ryan glanced down at the pictures. A feeling of exhilaration ran through him. The only lead they had was from a woman who'd glanced out her rear window and said she saw a real tall man going through her yard. It made sense. The pieces were beginning to fall into place. That's all Ryan had been waiting for. He had the feeling now that the thing would be busted wide open soon.

Benson began to put the books back together. "I hope you ain't trying to shit us, boy," he said, but he too couldn't hide the excitement in himself. He too felt that it was just a matter of time now. They had the hit men's names and pictures. Maybe they didn't have an eyewitness, but once they got their hands on these boys, they'd get a confession. One of them would crack. They always did.

"Well," Brown began slowly, "you guys goin' keep your word?" he asked, hinting about his twenty dollars.

Ryan could see his partner's lips turn down in a sneer, and he knew that Benson was about to say something that they might regret later on. The informer had come through for them, so he might come through again in the future. It was well worth the price of twenty dollars to get a line on the hit men.

"It's worth it, Benson," he said quickly. "Brown here really earned his pay. Let's split it up. Who knows, he might come up with something else one day that we might be able to use."

Benson didn't like the idea of paying out any money but, as Ryan said, it was sure worth it. "Okay give it to him. I'll give you my share as soon as we go out. I got to get some change for a twenty."

"I don't know if I got that much on me, Ben. So

you give him your twenty and I'll straighten with you, okay?"

Gritting his teeth, Benson set the books back down. He fumbled around to get his wallet out, then removed a twenty-dollar bill. "That was my fuckin' lunch money for the rest of this week, Ryan. I hate to see that bastard take it and shoot it up!"

"Don't let it worry you. I know Sally will give you a few more dollars if you should get uptight," Ryan said, referring to Benson's wife.

"Yeah," Benson replied, but he wasn't smiling. He didn't like the idea of paying informers. He tossed the twenty-dollar bill down on top of the desk. "Don't have an overdose with it, Brown," he stated coldly.

As he gathered up the large mug containers Ryan watched his partner. The hunched over shoulders and the firmly tightened jaw muscles revealed the man's feelings more than any words could. Ryan decided to get rid of Brown as soon as possible.

"What's wrong with him?" Brown asked as he was led from the room. "You wouldn't think that I just gave him the information that might get him a promotion, would you?" Brown was just paying lip service now. What he wanted most was to get as far away from the police station as he could. He would make his phone call from the nearest phone booth, then have King Fisher's men meet him somewhere. He wished there was some way he could get to meet the King Fisher in person. That would really be something. He would be set for life then. Anytime you worked for a man as big as the King Fisher you had to handle big cash. *How, how, how,* the thought kept flashing through his mind. If only he could set up an appointment, he felt sure he could sell himself to the man.

"Okay, Brown, now you keep in touch, hear?" Ryan said as they reached the elevator.

"Don't worry about me, man. Just check your partner out. I hate to work for people that don't appreciate what I'm doing. I could get killed for this shit, whether or not you guys realize it. I mean, your buddy has his fuckin' mouth pushed out over twenty dollars, yet I put my life on Front Street to help you guys out. I ain't gettin' no credit for this shit. I'm just doing you a favor, you know what I mean?"

Damn, Ryan said to himself stepping back so that he wouldn't have the man talking directly in his face. Brown's breath stank like yesterday's turds. Another good smell of it and he'd feel like letting up his lunch.

When the elevator came Ryan changed his mind about riding downstairs with the man. "Okay, Brown, I'll let you go from here. You know your way out. Now, next time, do it just like you did today. Don't worry about the money. If you have something nice we can use, I'll find the cash somewhere." Ryan held the door open and then stepped back before Brown could talk directly in his face.

James Brown only nodded his head in agreement. "Yeah, man, I'll just do that," he said, but his thoughts were completely different. It will be a cold day in hell before you bastards get some more information out of me, he reflected. If I hadn't needed to see that mug book, you motherfuckers wouldn't have got that info. He watched the door close, keeping the fake smile on his face until it was completely closed. Then he spit against the door. "You bastards," he cursed loudly, since he was the only one in the elevator. As soon as it reached the ground, he rushed towards the nearest phone booth How, oh how he wished he could have gotten his hands on a snapshot of those two guys.

Briefly he wondered how he could go about getting one of the pictures. He knew the men were ex-cons. There had to be other pictures of the men around. His mind raced, trying to figure out how it could be done. If he went back upstairs after the detectives left, could he possibly con one of the police-women into letting him glance back through the books? Naw, the bitches wouldn't go for it. After all, they were police too, even though the cunts had pussies.

Both of the phone booths were in use. He waited for a minute, then decided to find a booth outside. Brown almost ran out the door. He spotted one across the street, then almost got a ticket for jaywalking. He searched in his pockets frantically for the number.

King Fisher's men had been up on the corner passing out the number, telling everyone that the reward would be paid instantly. Finally Brown found what he was looking for. Then he had trouble finding a dime. For a second he thought he might have to go back across the street and get change for the twenty-dollar bill.

He finally found the dime, dropped the coin in the box, and dialed the number. Just as quickly he got a busy tone. He tried it again, and on the second try he got through.

"Hey man, this is Brown. Brown off of John R Street. Yeah, well I'm calling about that reward King Fisher is offering. Yeah, man, I'd like to see the King Fisher."

"Yeah, brother. I guess you would like to see the King Fisher," the man's voice came back over the phone. "You and half the niggers in the city. Now tell me, man, what have you got?"

"Hey, baby," Brown cried, "it don't go like that. I'm calling about the reward money, man, so take this off. Whoever you got to get in touch with, ask them how much will they pay for the names of the two men that made the hit?"

The man on the other end of the line got serious. Sam had leaned on him and the rest of the boys. They wanted this shit cleared up, and this might be the break he was looking for. "Listen, Brown, give me that number and I'll get right back to you."

"Okay, brother, 366-8247. But listen, my man, find out how much they're paying for the names, hear? I can't give you the guys' addresses, but I can sure tell you where they hang out at."

"Okay, Brown, just hold on, man." The line went dead in his ear, and in three minutes the phone rang. "Brown here," he said into the receiver.

"Listen, Brown, I'm going to send a car to pick you up. Where are you at?"

Brown hesitated for a minute. "Hey, Brown, how do you expect to pick up your money, man, if we don't do business with each other in person?" the voice asked.

"Okay, my man," Brown answered quickly, "how about pickin' me up on the corner of Brush and Vernor Highway? How long will it take?"

"We're leaving now, man. We'll be in a black Caddie, so when you see it cruise up, you'll know it's us. Oh yeah, Brown. Don't let this be no bullshit, man, 'cause we ain't got time for games."

"Don't worry about...." The phone went dead in Brown's ear. He hung it up and started walking. He figured that, by the time he got there, they should be pulling up. He was right. He hadn't been on the corner five minutes when a black Cadillac came up and stopped. Brown glanced at the two men sitting in the car as he walked up. Well, he told himself, here goes everything. They shouldn't do anything to me, he reasoned, since I got the information they want. Maybe I'll really get a chance to see the King Fisher after all.

As he neared the car the door opened; the man on the passenger side got out and got in back. "You Brown?" the man asked as he came up.

He could only nod his head in agreement. "Get in!" It was more like an order than anything else. The car pulled away from the curb before he could get the door closed tight.

"What's the guys' names?" the question came harshly.

"How much cash is involved, man?" Brown countered.

"I done told you once, Brown, that we don't play games. Now, who were the motherfuckers who knocked off David?"

The feel of cold blue steel against his neck started Brown to sweating.

"Brown, we ain't joking with you, man. We want them names!"

The gun pressed against his neck scared him, but the thought of the large reward being taken from him gave him courage. "Hey man, I heard the King Fisher was a for-real dude. The word is out that he is paying a reward for this information, man, and I want my share of it. Now, if you guys are trying to shake me down, I'm sorry. Killing me ain't goin' get the information for you."

Brown couldn't have told himself where he got the

nerve from, but it was there. "I want to see some
green, man, real paper. You dig where I'm coming
from? The cats I'm about to tell on would bury my
ass if they knew I was there, man."

Tim was just a leg man. Sam had told him to try
to shake the information out of the man but not to
blow it. Sam was on his way over to meet them so
that he could handle it himself. He had the cash with
him.

The driver, Big John, didn't say anything. Brown
glanced out of the window. He was surprised to see
them crossing the Belle Isle Bridge. They continued
on around the island until Big John parked near the
beach. As soon as they arrived, another Cadillac
pulled in behind them.

A big man wearing an expensive suit got out of the
passenger side and walked down toward a park table
near the water. Tom motioned for Brown to get out
and walk, then he came out behind Brown. He led the
way over to the tall brown-skinned man.

"Hi, Sam, this here is Brown. He says he's got the
info we want."

Sam spread his hankie and sat on the edge of the
table. "You wouldn't really be trying to run no game
on us, would you, boy?" he asked harshly, as he studied Brown. "You use, don't you?" The question took
Brown by surprise.

"Yeah, man, but I ain't sick, and I ain't broke. I got
enough for a fix, man, so this ain't no game."

"Let's see your bread," Sam ordered.

Brown removed the twenty-dollar bill, plus seven
more that he already had. He thanked his lucky stars that
he had shaken the police down for the twenty dollars.

"It ain't much," Sam stated as he examined Brown

closely. "I don't know, boy, you just might be silly enough to try a shakedown."

"No way, man. My maw ain't had no fools. Can't you see, brother, I ain't no kid? Man, I've been around a long time, so I must have some kind of brain," Brown managed to say.

"What's the name of these punks that made the hit?" Sam asked sharply.

There were tears of desperation in Brown's eyes but he shook his head. "Man, the wire said the big man was paying a reward; now, I don't have to get all of it, but I ain't givin' up what I know for nothin'. I just ain't goin' do it. Them cats would kill me if they knowed I was here, so I wanna see some kind of bread!"

Sam examined him closely. He was pretty good at reading human nature, but he also knew a junkie could lie to Jesus and get away with it. "How do I know these guys you're talking about did it?" Sam asked, then added, "How the fuck do you know if they really did it unless you was up on the hit?"

Brown choked back a lump in his throat, then said, "I'm goin' tell you what I know, then see if you believe the names are worth anything." Then he ran it down how he had watched them following David for the past week. When he finished he told everything except the names.

"And you say you know these motherfuckers' names, huh?" For the first time Brown told a lie. "I was in the joint with them. They don't know me but I know them. This one guy played on the prison basketball team," Brown said easily.

Sam shook his head. It sounded like these were his people all right. He believed he would have been able to see through lies if Brown hadn't been telling the truth. Yet he didn't know where they lived, which made sense too. Hit men wouldn't run around telling people how to get in touch with them, but Brown knew what neighborhood they hung out in. All young blacks have to have somewhere to hang out and brag.

"Tell me something, Brown. Do you think your information is worth five grand?" Sam asked quietly.

Brown shook his head. "It may not be worth that kind of money, but it's worth something, mister."

Sam pulled out his roll and peeled off two one-hundred-dollar bills. "How about that?" he inquired in that cold voice of his.

"That should just about pay for the neighborhood they hang out in," Brown replied, seeing the huge roll and realizing that it was up to him to talk his way into as much money as he could get. "I not only know the two men's names, I also know their nicknames," Brown stated, wetting his lips. They had become so dry that he found it hard to talk. "So I'll ask you in all honesty, don't you think that's worth more than what you're offering me?"

Sam looked at the man and laughed. "If you weren't a hype, Brown, I could have used you. Now, give me some information that I can use." He wasn't asking anymore.

Brown didn't bother reaching for the money. "I'm goin' put all my cards on the table with you, man, and hope you'll give me a fair shake. I don't know how much it's worth to you. Only you can be the judge of that."

How much it's worth to me, Sam thought to himself. It's worth my home, my car, my wife, my very life. That's what it's worth, but he never showed it as he talked. King Fisher wanted the men who had done this, and if he didn't get them he was going to replace a lot of people, starting with Sam.

Sam made a gesture with his hand. "Let's hear it, Brown. I ain't goin' try and fuck you out of no money. If I think your information is good, I'll pay you accordingly."

"Okay," Brown said. "The short one's name is Billy Good and the tall one is Jackie Walker, I think. But anyway, they're called 'Mutt' and 'Jeff,' 'cause one's so tall while the other one is so short. They hang out on the north end.

Sam stood up so quickly that he took Brown by surprise. "Get on the phone," he said to one of his men, "and call Bennie's barbershop. Ask him for the lowdown on a couple of punks called 'Mutt and Jeff,' then ask him what their names are."

The man hurried over to the car Sam had got out of and started talking on the phone. He was back in a few minutes, smiling. "He knew who I was talking about, Sam. The two studs are supposed to be pretty good stickup men, and there are a few wires out on them as hit men, even though their business is generally kept quiet. Dangerous is the word," Bennie said.

"What about their names?" Sam asked, snapping his fingers. "Did you forget to ask?"

"Naw, I got them, Sam. Uh, let me think a second. Oh yeah, Billy and Jackie. He didn't know their last names, but those are the first ones."

Sam smiled broadly, but the smile didn't reach his eyes. He was sure they had their men. It was just a matter of time now. "Go back and tell Bennie to get a line on where the two of them stay," he ordered and waited until the man left. "I guess you did earn a little more than two hundred, Brown," he said and began counting. When he reached five hundred he stopped.

Brown couldn't believe his luck. At first it had just been an idea, but it had paid off. Five hundred. He had never expected the five grand. The five hundred was like five grand. But as he watched, Sam peeled off some more bills. He put ten one-hundred-dollar bills in Brown's hand.

"How's that, Brown? Does that make you happy?"

Brown could only shake his head. "Happy" wasn't the word. He didn't know how to thank Sam. Sam just waved him down, not wanting to hear it.

"That's all right, brother," Sam said as he got up from the table. "I am very thankful for the information you gave us. If you want, my boys will drop you off at the nearest bus stop. And don't shoot too much dope at once, Brown. You might not live to enjoy your good luck." His laughter rang out loud and clear as he headed for his Cadillac.

13

Billy and Jackie ended up staying out at the farm until the day before the robbery. Then they decided to come back to the city. Billy had made one trip in earlier that week, to take Joy over to her mother's house, where he had met her parents and played with her young child. The little boy was only four years old, but he had taken to the big man right off.

The people on the farm who weren't working that day gathered in the driveway and waved good-bye to the group as they left. Billy was taking Joy back to his place. They had decided to try living together. After the holdup, Billy planned on taking a trip to New York.

They had an uneventful trip back to the city. "In a way, I hate to come back here," Billy stated as he pulled up and parked in front of their apartment.

"Yeah, I know what you mean," Jackie replied as he waited impatiently for Joy to get out. His long legs were cramped from the small space in the rear of the car. "After this, Billy, we're going to have to start renting larger cars."

Having never been over to the apartment, Joy didn't know which way to go, so she just stood on the sidewalk and waited for Billy to come around the car. She noticed the three black men get out of the parked car and start towards them, but she didn't really pay any attention to them until they were on top of the small crowd gathering on the sidewalk.

Her first warning came when she heard Jackie call out, "Look out, Billy, they got guns." At the sound of his yell, she glanced up in time to see what looked like a short stick come from under one of the men's suitcoats. Then the street lit up with noise. Billy brought a pistol from under his coat, but it was too late.

He let out a cry of pain when he saw Joy fall to the sidewalk, blood running from a large hole in her neck. She never even managed to scream. Then he was lifted off his feet and hurled backwards. He heard Jackie scream, "The bastard's using a sawed-off shotgun!"

From his knees Billy tried to raise the pistol in his hand, but another blow struck him, spinning him around. The sidewalk came up and met him, even as Jackie started to crumble. He had been a little more lucky. He managed to get off two shots before the shotgun blew the life out of him. Carol screamed and started to run. A blow in her back knocked her off her feet. She crawled a few more feet on the sidewalk, leaving a bloody trail, until another well-placed bullet took her out of her misery. She fell over on the sidewalk, face down.

The people glancing out of their windows saw a rare sight, even for a ghetto—two black men and two black women dead on the sidewalk. Even as they watched, a black Cadillac with three men in it pulled away from the curb. Their job had been well done. The Big Man could sleep nights again.

Maybe.

Donald Goines
SPECIAL PREVIEW

DADDY COOL

This excerpt from Daddy Cool *will introduce you to Larry Jackson, who is better known to his clients as "Daddy Cool"—and they know he is the best. He can pull a trigger or toss a knife and never blink an eye. All that counts is the bread—and his teenage daughter, Janet. But when Janet is enticed into his stable by a young, smooth-talking pimp named Ronald, Daddy Cool sees red—and goes into action with a fearful vengeance!*

Larry Jackson, better known as "Daddy Cool," stopped on the litter-filled street in the town of Flint, Michigan. His prey, a slim, brown-complexioned man, walked briskly ahead. He was unaware that he was being followed by one of the deadliest killers the Earth had ever spawned.

Taking his time, Daddy Cool removed a cigarette pack and lit up a Pall Mall. He wasn't in any hurry, he knew that the frightened man in front of him was as good as dead. Whenever the man glanced back over his shoulder he saw nothing moving on the dark side of the street.

William Billings let out a sigh of relief. He had got-

ten away with it. Everybody had talked about how
relentless the numbers barons were that he worked for,
but after ten years of employment with the numbers
men, he had come to the conclusion that it was just
another business. Like the well-talked-about Mafia,
the black numbers men he worked for depended on
their reputations to carry them along. And many of
those frightening stories out of the past became so out-
rageous that separating reality from unreality often
was impossible.

Five years ago William had formulated the idea of
how to rip off the people he worked for, but it had
taken him another five years to get up the nerve to
really put his dream to work. It had been easier than
he imagined. The money had just been lying there,
waiting for him to pick it up. Actually, he was the
accountant, so every day he was in contact with at
least ten thousand dollars in cash. The problem lay
with faking out the two elderly women who worked
in the storefront with him. William had to hold back
a burst of laughter when he went back over the events
and how simple it had been. All those years of waiting, being afraid of what might happen if he walked
out with the money, had made him ashamed. He could
have ripped off the money five years earlier and been
in South America by now, with his dream ranch pro-
ducing money. But out of fear he had waited. Now
that he had done it, he realized that all the waiting
had been in vain. It had only been his inborn fear that
had kept him from being rich.

A young girl in her early teens walked past, her
short skirt revealing large, meaty thighs. William did
something he never did. He spoke to the young girl
as she went past, her hips swaying enticingly.

The girl ignored the older balding man, keeping her head turned sideways so that she didn't have to look into his leering eyes.

At any other time the flat rejection would have filled William with a feeling of remorse. But now, because of the briefcase he carried, it didn't faze him at all. He even managed to let out a contemptuous laugh. The silly fool, he coldly reflected. If she had only known that I carried enough money in this brief-case to make every dream she ever had come true, she wouldn't have acted so funky. He laughed again, the sound carrying to the young girl as she hurried on her way home. At the sound of William's laughter she began to walk faster. His laughter seemed to be sinister in the early evening darkness that was quickly falling. The sudden appearance of another man from around a parked car gave the girl a fright, but after another quick glance, she forgot about him. It was obvious that the man wasn't paying any attention to her. She glanced back once at the tall black man, then hurried on her way.

At the sight of the young girl coming down the street Daddy Cool pulled his short-brimmed hat farther down over his eyes. He didn't want anyone recognizing him at this particular moment.

At the sound of Billings' voice, Daddy Cool relaxed. If William could find anything to laugh about at this stage of the game, it showed that the man was shaking off the fear that had made him so cautious earlier in the day. Now it was just a matter of the right opportunity presenting itself. Then Daddy Cool could take care of his job and be on his way home in a matter of moments.

At the thought of home, a slight frown crossed

Larry's face. His wife would be cuddled up in the bed watching the television at this time of night. Janet might be anywhere. Without him at home she would surely run wild, staying out to daybreak before coming home, because she knew their mother would be sound asleep by the time she came in. And even if she was awake, there was nothing to fear, because she wouldn't say anything to her about keeping late hours. All she was interested in was having a cold bottle of beer in her hand and a good television program. That was what made her happy.

Larry frowned in the dark as he wondered about the tricks fate could play on a man. He remembered the first time he had seen his wife. She had been dancing with a group at a small nightclub. How he had wished he could make her his woman. Now, twenty years later, after getting the woman he had dreamed about as a young man, he realized just how foolish he had been. Instead of choosing a woman for her brains, he had foolishly chosen one because of the way she was built. The last fifteen years had been lived regretting his ignorance.

Even as he followed this line of thought, he realized that he would have put her out long ago if it hadn't been for his daughter, Janet. Knowing how it was to grow up as a child without any parents, he had sworn to raise any children born to him. Janet had been the only child born out of his marriage. So he had poured out all his love for his only child, giving Janet whatever she thought about having. He had spoiled the girl before she was five years old. Now that she was in her teens, he couldn't remember when either one of them had ever whipped the child. Janet had grown up headstrong and used to having her way.

Because of the money Daddy Cool made, it hadn't bothered him. Whatever the child had ever wanted, he had been able to give it to her.

Daddy Cool noticed the man he was following turn the corner and start walking faster. There was no better time than now to make the hit. As long as the man stayed on these back streets it would be perfect. He only had to catch up with the man without arousing his suspicions. Daddy Cool started to lengthen his stride until he was almost running.

William had a definite goal. A longtime friend stayed somewhere in the next block, but over the years he had forgotten just where the house was. In his haste to leave Detroit, he had left his address book on the dining-room table, so it was useless to him now. He slowed down, knowing that he would recognize the house when he saw it. It was on Newal Street, that he was sure of. It shouldn't be too hard to find in the coming darkness.

Like a hunted animal, Billings' nerves were sharpened to a peak. Glancing back over his shoulder, he noticed a tall man coming around the corner. His first reaction was one of alarm. His senses, alert to possible danger, had detected the presence of someone or something in the immediate vicinity. As a shiver of fear ran down his spine he ridiculed himself for being frightened of his own shadow. There was no need for him to be worried about someone picking up his trail. Not this soon anyway.

Disregarding the warning alarm that went off inside his head, he slowed his pace so that he could see the old shabby houses better. The neighborhood had once been attractive, with the large rambling homes built back in the early twenties. But now, they were crum-

bling. Most of them needed at least a paint job. Where
there had once been rain gutters, there were now only
rusted-out pieces of tin, ready to collapse at the first
burst of rain.

William cursed under his breath. He wondered if,
in his early haste, he might have made a wrong turn.
It was possible. It had been years since he had been
up this way, and it was easy for him to get turned
around. He slowed his walk down until he was almost
standing still. Idly, he listened to the footsteps of the
man who had turned down the same street as he did.
Unable to control himself, William turned completely around and glanced at the tall, somberly dressed
man coming toward him. He let out a sigh as he realized that he had been holding his breath. He noticed
that the man coming toward him was middle-aged.
Probably some family man, he reasoned, hurrying
home from work. He almost laughed out loud as he
reflected on what a hired killer would look like. He
was sure of one thing, a hit man wouldn't be as old
as the man coming toward him. In his mind, William
pictured the hit man sent out after him as a wild young
man, probably in his early twenties. A man in a hurry
to make a name for himself. One who didn't possess
too high an intelligence, that being the reason he
would have become a professional killer. It didn't take
any brains to pull the trigger on a gun, William reasoned. But a smart man would stay away from such
an occupation. One mistake and a hit man's life was
finished.

Suddenly William decided that he was definitely
going the wrong way. He whirled around on his heels
swiftly. The tall, light-complexioned man coming near
him stopped suddenly. For a brief moment William

hesitated, thinking he saw fear on the man's face. The dumb punk-ass bastard, William coldly reflected. If the sorry motherfucker only knew how much cash William had in the briefcase he carried, the poor bastard wouldn't be frightened by William's sudden turn.

"Don't worry, old chap," William said loudly so that the other man wouldn't fear him. "I'm just lost, that's all. These damn streets all look alike at night."

The tall, dark-clothed man had hesitated briefly; now he came forward quickly. He spoke softly "Yeah, mister, you did give me a fright for just a minute. You know," he continued, as he approached, "you can't trust these dark streets at night. Some of these dope fiends will do anything for a ten-dollar bill."

William laughed lightly, then smiled. He watched the tall man reach back behind his collar. Suddenly the smile froze on his face as the evening moonlight sparkled brightly off the keen-edged knife that was twitching in the man's hand.

Without thinking, William held out his hand. "Wait a minute," he cried out in fear. "If it's money you want, I'll give you all mine." Even in his fright William tried to hold onto the twenty-five thousand dollars he had in the briefcase. He reached for the wallet in his rear pocket. He never reached it.

With a flash the tall man dressed in black threw his knife. The motion was so smooth and quick that the knife became only a blur. The knife seemed to turn in the air once or twice, then become imbedded in William's slim chest. It happened so suddenly that William never made a sound. The force of the blow staggered him. He remained on his feet for a brief instant with the knife protruding from his body.

With a quiet groan, William Billings began to fall.

The pavement struck him in the back. His eyes were open slightly as he felt more than saw the silent man bending down over him. He tried to open his eyes wider as he felt the knife being withdrawn. Why? he wanted to ask, but the question never formed on his lips. The cold steel against his neck was the last thing he felt on this Earth. When the tall, light-complexioned man stood up with the briefcase hanging limp from his left hand, William Billings never heard the quiet words the man spoke.

"You should have never tried to take it, friend," Daddy Cool said as he leaned down and wiped the blood off his favorite dagger. He liked to use the knives whenever he could. They were quieter and less trouble. He glanced back over his shoulder to see if anybody had noticed the silent affair. The streets were still deserted, as the cool evening breeze began to blow.

Without another glance, Daddy Cool stepped to the curb and quickly crossed the street. His long strides took him away from the murder scene quickly. He walked briskly but not so much in a hurry as to draw attention. When he reached the corner, he took a backward glance and for the first time noticed an old black woman coming down the steps from the shabby house where the body lay.

At the sight of him peering back at her, she hesitated and stood where she was.

"Damn!" The curse exploded from Daddy Cool's lips as his jaw muscles drew tight. The old bitch had probably been watching the whole thing from her darkened windows. But, Daddy Cool reasoned as he continued on his way, it had been too dark for her to see anything. No matter. He began to move swiftly now toward his car, which was parked two blocks away on another side street.

Daddy Cool turned down the next block and silently cut through somebody's yard. He walked quietly, listening for dogs. His luck held as he made it through the yard and didn't run into any dogs until he started to cut through a yard that he was sure would bring him out near his car. Now his mind was busy. He wondered if the old bitch had called the police before coming out and trying to give aid to a dead man. If she had, they would be setting up lookouts for a man on foot. He couldn't take any more chances.

The large, muscular German police dog jumped up on the fence and barked loudly. Daddy Cool took a quick glance at the house and noticed that it was dark. There was the chance that everybody was sound asleep, but he doubted it. They were more than likely watching television. He started to walk down to the next yard but instantly saw that the yard contained two large mongrel dogs. Without hesitating, Daddy Cool retraced his steps.

Again the large German police dog jumped up against the fence, barking loudly. Suddenly his bark stopped and the dog toppled back on the ground with the handle of the long dagger sticking out of his neck. Daddy Cool took the time to retrieve his knife. He couldn't leave it. It was like a calling card. If the police found his knife they would know that a professional had been at work. Over the past years, he had had to leave his knives on three different occasions. His knives were handmade by him in his own basement, so that there was no way of tracing them to any stores. But the police in three different cities had his knives, waiting for a day when they would be able to tie them with the killer who so boldly used them. For the past ten years certain detectives followed up all knife killings such as the one that had been committed tonight. With patience they slowly waited until one day the killer would make a mistake.

Daddy Cool didn't have the slightest intention of making that mistake. The thought of driving all the way back home with the telltale knife in his possession was a grim thought. If the police should stop him and find the knife, he would be busted. As he crossed the yard silently, he removed his handkerchief and wiped the knife clean. Then, seeing that the back steps of the porch were open underneath, he leaned down and tossed the knife and hankie under the house as far as he could.

Without seeming to have stopped, he continued on his silent way, coming out on the sidewalk and quickly walking past two houses to where his black Ford was parked. He tossed the briefcase on the seat beside him and started up the car motor. Glancing up, he saw the headlights of a car turn down the block, and he quickly cut his motor off and stretched out on the car seat. As soon as he heard the car pass, he raised up and watched it go on down the street. With patience, he waited until the headlights disappeared completely before restarting his own car.

He pulled out onto the deserted street and drove silently toward the main street, which would lead eventually to the highway.

2

It took less than an hour after arriving back in Detroit for Daddy Cool to take care of his business. The first thing he did was to drop off the briefcase with the twenty-five thousand dollars. He received his ten-thousand-dollar payment for the contract, then started for home. It was three o'clock in the morning when he turned off Seven Mile Road and drove slowly down Ripelle Street. The neighborhood was still mixed but was quickly becoming predominantly black. The homes were well taken care of because the blacks in the neighborhood had paid top dollar to purchase the high-priced homes from the fleeing whites. The well-kept lawns gleamed brightly in the moonlight.

Daddy Cool had a feeling of pride as he drove slowly up to his expensive ranch-style home. He had it built from the ground up, after first putting his money into a poolroom so that he could give the appearance of being a smart businessman. He had been around too long to fall into the trap that many of the other money-hungry blacks fell into: buying high-priced homes with no apparent means of support.

The circular driveway was always a source of pride to him, but now, as he pulled into it, his lips tightened into a snarl. The long, powder-blue Cadillac parked in front of the carport brought his anger to the boiling point. He knew at once who the car belonged to. It was one of the young boys in the neighborhood who thought of himself as a pimp. Many times Daddy Cool had sat in his poolroom and listened to this same young man talk about his exploits with the young girls of the neighborhood. Now the young man was spending his time with Janet, Daddy Cool's young daughter. He had warned the girl about the boy, but she hadn't paid any attention to him, thinking he was just being old-fashioned. She loved the attention she received when she and the self-proclaimed pimp rode through the neighborhood with the top down.

Pulling up behind the car, Daddy Cool sat quietly behind the wheel, using the time to gain some control of his temper. He had never let any of his children see him in a rage, and he had no intention of losing it now. He remembered his only close friend, Big Earl, begging him to let him handle the young punk who was so disrespectful. Daddy Cool had laughingly put the massive black man off. Earl was several inches taller than Daddy Cool, who himself stood over six feet. As Daddy Cool thought about his friend's quiet request, he couldn't help picturing the massive black with his oversized head. Even for his huge body, Earl's head was too large—it was deformed and roughly the girth and shape of a young watermelon. His eyes were bulbous and froglike. A vivid pale scar ran from his forehead to his neck, cutting his face into two unequal halves. Both of his ears had missing lobes, and what remained had healed unevenly.

The man was grotesque, to say the least, and he brought fear to many who saw him for the first time. His only desire was to serve Daddy Cool, who gave him a place to stay behind the poolroom and a job that kept him off the streets. For that his loyalty was complete. He would freely give his life for the tall, light-complexioned man who accepted him so freely without question.

Now the thought of this huge man's desire to take care of the young pimp named Ronald brought a slight smile to Daddy Cool's face, but he didn't really need big Earl to do anything for him. He could take care of Ronald himself. If he ever made up his mind to do it.

As he stared ahead at the parked Cadillac, he knew the boy had seen his headlights when he pulled up. But Ronald had made no attempt to pull out of his way. Instead, Ronald had wrapped his arms around Janet and kissed her slowly. Finally, having watched too much, Daddy Cool pressed down on his horn, blowing it loudly as he again fought down his boiling temper. The young pimp was thoroughly dislikable. He seemed to go out of his way to antagonize Daddy Cool.

With slow deliberation, Ronald started the motor of his car as Janet jumped out on the passenger side. She waved and smiled brightly at Ronald, then whirled

around on her heels. Her lips came down into a frown,
and Daddy Cool knew that she was angry. He took a
quick glance at his watch and noticed that it was
almost three-thirty in the morning. That was one hell
of a time for a girl just sixteen to be coming home.
Although she was on the verge of turning seventeen,
she was still a child to him.

Janet waited with her hands on her hips while her
father pulled up and parked under the car shed. Daddy
Cool sighed as he got out. His anger was going to be
his downfall one day if he didn't learn to control it
better. Even as he approached the girl he cautioned
himself about his anger. His temper was already
almost out of control and he didn't really know how
much he could take. From the happenings of the past
night's work, he was still keyed up to a high pitch.
He tried to slow himself down.

"Well!" Janet snarled like a young jungle cat. Her
bright teeth gleamed in the moonlight. She was a
bewitching picture standing there with her hands on
her hips. Her hair was long and silky, running down
to her shoulders like shining black silver. Her face had
a golden tone to it, more Mexican than Negro. Her
lips were thin, like her father's, and she had the same
leaping black eyes, which looked like those of wild
hawks with their eyes gleaming under the moonlight.

"You know you didn't have to do that, Daddy," she
began. "We knew it was you pulling up behind us.
Ronald only wanted to say good night to me without
pulling away at your sudden appearance as if he was
frightened. I mean, he's a man, too, even if he is much
younger than you."

It wasn't so much the words she used that hurt him,
it was the tone of voice. She spoke to him as if she

was scolding a child. Before he knew what he was doing, his hand came up and knocked her to the ground. She stared up at him in surprise. This was the first time he had ever put his hands on her, and she couldn't believe that it had happened. Before she could say anything sassy he reached down and jerked her to her feet.

"Hear this, little bitch," he growled, and he didn't recognize his own voice. "If you ever try speakin' to me in that tone of voice again, I'll kick your ass so hard you won't be able to sit sideways in that goddamn Caddie, you understand?"

Before she could shake her head one way or the other his hand moved in a blur. Twice he slapped her viciously across the face. Her scream came out shrilly at first, then louder. He twisted her around and gave her a violent shove toward the front door.

"And another thing, Miss Fine, as long as you live under this goddamn roof, you had better make sure that motherfuckin' door hits you in the crack of your ass before twelve o'clock at night," he stated, then added, "Do I make myself clear?"

Janet could only nod her head. She was too frightened to speak. She had never really seen the man who was walking swiftly behind her. This wasn't the soft old man she could bend around her fingers like putty. No, this was another person, one whom she had never seen before. For the first time in her life she feared the man who had always been dear to her. She trembled as she hurried toward the front door. With shaking hands she inserted her key and quickly opened the front door.

Tears ran freely from her eyes as she staggered across the threshold. As Daddy Cool entered, the first thing he noticed was his wife, to whose arms Janet had fled.

"Oh, Mother," she cried over and over again.

"Now, now, child," Daddy Cool's wife, Shirley, said. "It's okay, honey. Everything is all right." Her eyes sought out those of her husband. The sounds from in front of their house had awakened her, but she had no knowledge of what had happened to her daughter.

"He struck me," Janet finally managed to say, as large tears ran down both her cheeks. A sob caught in her throat as she remembered the vivid scene that had just transpired.

Shirley was dumbfounded. She didn't have the slightest idea of who her daughter was talking about. It never even entered her mind that Daddy Cool was the one she was referring to.

"Larry," Shirley said, addressing her husband sharply, "what is this child talking about?"

"She tryin' to tell you that I slapped her," Larry Jackson stated, as he stared cold-eyed at his wife.

"What!" Shirley exclaimed loudly, unable to catch up with the conversation. She couldn't believe what she had heard.

"I said she is tryin' to pull your coat that I slapped the shit out of her," Daddy Cool stated harshly.

"You slapped her?" Shirley murmured over and over again. Even now that the words were out Shirley still couldn't believe that she had heard right.

"That's right," he stated again. "If you had taken care of your responsibilities like you should have, this wouldn't have been necessary. I told you before I left to stay on this kid's ass and make her come home early!"

"Shit!" The word came out louder than she had intended. Shirley dropped her eyes. She didn't like the cold gleam that came into her man's jet black eyes. "I mean, Larry, you know she won't mind me. Hell, if she won't mind you, how the hell do you expect me to make her mind me?"

With firm hands Shirley slowly disengaged herself from her daughter.

"Okay now, Janet, it's all right. It won't kill you. Maybe it might slow you down some though." She gently pushed her daughter away.

Finally Janet stopped crying. The tears stopped flowing and anger began to overwhelm her. For the first time in her young life she was speechless. She had been slapped, and to her that was something unheard of. As the thought of what had happened dawned on her, her cheeks became red with a futile anger.

"Mother," she began, then didn't really know what she wanted to say.

"Larry," Shirley said, "don't you think it's a late date to start using a strong hand on her?"

"Not as long as she keeps her young ass in my house," Daddy Cool stated harshly, his anger still not completely under control.

"Well, that's not so difficult to handle," Janet replied, sparks of fire leaping in her cold black eyes.

"What do you mean by that?" he asked softly. The gentleness of his voice hadn't fooled Shirley. She had lived with the man too long. She knew his moods almost as well as he did. She tried to catch her daughter's eye so that she could warn Janet, but the young girl was now in open rebellion. With her mother near, she believed she didn't have any reason to fear her

father. What had happened outside would never occur
in front of Shirley.

"What I mean," Janet said contemptuously, "is that
I don't just have to live here. I can easily find me a
small apartment somewhere." She shook her head
quickly, tossing the hair back out of her face.

"And just how the hell do you expect to pay the
rent, may I ask?" Daddy Cool asked quietly, watching his daughter closely. Each word she said seemed
to burn inside his head.

"That shouldn't be too hard either," Janet stated
coldly, her face flushed with anger.

"I suppose you think that punk Ronald is going to
pay your rent for you, huh?" Daddy Cool inquired.

"He just might at that," she said in a sassy manner,
while her mother let out a gasp.

"Larry," Shirley interrupted, "let's let this thing ride
until morning. Maybe after we sleep on it we can talk
about it with less heat, okay?" She stared from one
face to the other. They were so much alike, she reflected. Each one was strong-willed and neither one would
willingly give in. If only she could think of some way
to get them away from the conversation. Shirley saw
the danger that loomed ahead, while her husband was
too angry to realize that he was driving his daughter
up a one-way street with no way of getting back.

Daddy Cool let out a sharp laugh. "Yeah, I'll just
bet he'll pay out cash money for a place for you. By
the time you finished selling ass each and every night,
you'd have made enough money to pay the rent of a
penthouse!"

Janet let out a gasp. "Is that what you think?" She
stared at her father with hatred. "You don't think no
better of me than that," she stated again, not really

believing the words she heard.

"It's not you I believe in. It's that funky nigger you think you're playin' around with. He ain't nothing but a petty-ass pimp, so what makes you think you'll be treated any better than the rest of his girls?" Daddy Cool asked coldly, his jet black eyes flashing their anger.

Janet whirled around on her heels and stalked off toward her bedroom. Her stepbrother, Jimmy, stood in her path. There was a smile on his lips revealing that he had overheard most of the conversation.

"Would you mind getting out of my way?" she scowled in a scorching voice as she stared coldly at the tall, well-built boy.

"Yes ma'am," Jimmy said as he bowed from the waist, grinning. "Anything your highness might want, I'se the black boy to do it." He used a southern dialect that he knew would irritate his half sister.

"Get out of her way, Jimmy," Daddy Cool ordered, watching the exchange between the teenagers.

"Yes sirreee," Jimmy replied, jumping back quickly.

Shirley let out a sigh as she watched her daughter stalk off. This morning's work wouldn't be soon forgotten, she reflected as she watched Janet's proud back.

Shirley turned to her husband. "Well, Larry, I think you overplayed your hand that time, honey."

Daddy Cool didn't bother to answer. He waited until the girl disappeared, then he hurried to his bedroom.

3

The sunlight beaming through the framed bedroom window cast rays of gold on the bedspread. Normally, Daddy Cool would have been up by now. One quick look at his diamond-studded watch assured him of the time—it was a little past high noon. For him, it was rare indeed to stay in bed that long. The sunlight generally awakened him early in the morning. Then he would get up and take his morning shower. But today was different. His glance lingered on the ten thousand dollars lying on the dresser top. Most of the time this sight would lift his spirits. But today he couldn't pull his feelings together. Seldom did he allow himself to be down and blue, nor did he like to have anybody

around him who was in such a mood. So Daddy Cool
remained lying in bed, smoking cigarette after cigarette.

There was a soft knock on the door. "Who is it?"
Daddy Cool inquired sharply, more so than he had
actually intended.

Shirley hesitated, then spoke up.

"It's me, Larry," she said, then added, "I was wondering if you might like me to fix you something. I
could make you a ham sandwich right quick." Her
voice was shaking slightly.

Without even thinking about it, he almost dismissed
her. Then Daddy Cool remonstrated himself for being
so damn evil and changed his mind.

"Okay Shirley," he replied, trying to make the tone
of his voice casual. "I'm gettin' up now, so by the
time I take a fast shower, you can lay something out
for me. Oh, by the way, honey, if we don't have any,
send one of the boys down to the store and pick up
some cans of iced tea, okay?"

He didn't wait to hear her reply. Slipping off the
bed, he took off the silk shorts and walked naked into
the shower. After taking a cold shower he felt a little
better. He wondered idly if he was ducking his daughter. He remembered too vividly the events of the early
morning. Regret was written across his face as he
stared into the mirror. The last thing he should have
done, he scolded himself, was to allow his anger to
get away from him. Putting his hands on her was the
most foolish thing he'd done in years, he thought.

Taking his time, Daddy Cool selected the clothes
he would wear for the day. He was an excellent dresser for a man his age. Keeping up with the latest in
men's styles, he was always neat. Today he selected
a short, light brown silk shirt, then matched it with a

pair of brown pants with large cuffs. Next, he opened the closet where he kept over twenty pairs of shoes.

The latest were those with large heels and he removed a pair that he had only worn once before. The shoes were brown and white, with four-inch heels. He sprinkled powder inside the shoes before slipping his feet into them. Then he stood up and examined himself in the large bedroom mirror. He could find nothing wrong with his appearance.

He started for the door, then stopped and came back. Picking the stacks of money up from the top of the dresser, he opened his bottom drawer and casually dropped the money into it. After firmly closing it, he departed from the bedroom.

Shirley glanced up, smiling, when he entered the kitchen. The food was already on the table.

"I didn't know if you wanted to eat in here or in the dining room," she stated, as she wondered what kind of mood her man was in this morning.

"It don't make any difference," Larry stated as he pulled out a chair and sat down. He began to eat the ham sandwich, and once he'd done so he realized he was hungry. She watched him eating, then hurried and prepared him another one before he finished with the first. The cold tea had already been poured out of the can and was now in a glass with ice cubes. He drank the tea slowly, enjoying the light meal.

When Shirley bent down and set the food in front of him, Daddy Cool stared down at the well developed tits that pushed her blouse out so far in the front. He let out a sigh. His woman was still as attractive as ever. She had gained weight, but it looked good on her because it was all in the right places.

Shirley had the same golden brown complexion that

their daughter had, and also the beautiful and evenly spaced white teeth—something Daddy Cool knew he lacked. His teeth were disfigured and gaps could be seen whenever he opened his mouth.

"I'm glad to see you're in a better mood than you were this morning," Shirley began, slowly feeling her way. She knew that she had something to tell him, and she realized that once she told him his anger would shoot up to the boiling point.

"Well, let's just say that's left to be seen," he answered slowly, eyeing his wife closely for the first time that day. Something was on the woman's mind. He believed that he could read her like a book.

Before she could begin, he beat her to the point. "Ain't no sense bullshittin', Shirley. Whatever you got to say, spit it out." He stared at her coldly, knowing that whenever he looked at her in this fashion it upset her. Nevertheless, he didn't make it any easier for her.

Shirley rolled her tongue out and wet her lips, wildly trying to figure out which would be the best way to give her husband the news. Under his sharp stare she became confused and just blurted it out. "Your daughter had a cab pick her up this morning!"

Daddy Cool took a sip from his drink before replying. "So what? It ain't no big thing for her to catch a cab, is it?"

"No, no, not at all," Shirley began, still afraid to add the final words. But then it all came out in a rush. "But this is the first time she took all her clothes with her."

For a minute there was a deadly silence in the kitchen. Shirley could feel herself backing away from the table. The expression that flashed across her quiet husband's face frightened her. It was rare indeed when she saw him like this.

Once many years ago, when they had first gotten married, a man had accosted them in a bar and ignored Daddy Cool while trying to hold a conversation with her. She had seen that look then, before her husband had cut the man with his straight razor.

Daddy Cool had to repeat himself twice before his wife could understand what he was saying. She was so frightened that it was almost impossible to reach her.

"I said, bitch," he growled, "why the fuck didn't you wake me up and tell me what she was trying to pull off?"

Shirley shook her head in fear. "I didn't know myself, Larry. Jimmy told me about it when I got up. He said she left with three suitcases."

"Jimmy, huh!" Daddy Cool said the name with emphasis. "Just where the hell is Jimmy at now?"

"He went to basketball practice with his brother," she managed to reply.

There was a coldness in the room now and Shirley knew that she didn't have any influence on what her angry husband might do. No matter what she thought, he wouldn't pay the slightest heed to her demands.

Daddy Cool stared coldly at his wife. "I guess you don't really care one way or the other about this shit, do you, Shirley?"

"Of course I care," she answered quickly, "but there's not too much we can do. She'll be seventeen in another month, so we really don't have much control over her movements now. It's just too late, Larry. We should have taken this interest in her activities way before now."

For a brief second Larry felt like slapping his wife's face but realized that it wasn't completely her fault.

It was their joint mismanagement of the young girl's affairs that had led to this. Neither one had been firm enough, and now it was damn near too late. But Daddy Cool wouldn't allow himself to even think that it was actually too late.

He believed he could still do something to straighten the matter out. If he could only find her and sit down and have a good talk with her, then she would understand that everything he was doing was for her own good.

With his brain whirling beneath the stunning revelation, Daddy Cool sat rigid, unable to think properly. He couldn't bring his thoughts together; he couldn't make the proper moves.

"It's not just Jimmy's fault," Shirley stated, then added, "Buddy was up and he saw her packing her stuff, so he could have awakened you as well as Jimmy."

Without really realizing what he was saying, Daddy Cool replied, "Since Buddy and Jimmy ain't nothing but her half brothers, they both were more than likely glad to see her go. That way," he continued, "they probably hope that they'll be able to get more spending money from me."

Shirley caught her breath. She had known for years that her husband only tolerated her two boys from another man, but this was the first time he had ever said something openly about it. It wasn't what he said, but the way that he said it.

"I guess, then," Shirley began, "it wouldn't make any damn difference to you if Buddy or Jimmy were leaving."

Daddy Cool laughed harshly. "I should say not. Why in the fuck should I be concerned? I've raised

them and given them any goddamn thing they ever
wanted, so now that both of them are grown, do you
think I'd shed tears if they decided to leave?"

He gazed up at her with wide, unseeing eyes. He
could only see his young daughter in his mind.

Gradually Shirley fought back the tears that were
slowly building. "I don't know why you want to say
they're grown. Jimmy is only eighteen, while Buddy
is just a year older than that."

The thought raced through Daddy Cool's mind. He
pushed his chair back from the table. "If you want to
baby them boys, that's up to you. But don't think for
a goddamn minute I'm going to baby them also. When
I was sixteen I was out on my own, and I think it
made a better man out of me. Your boys are both
spoiled little bastards who are used to havin' their own
fuckin' way because I made it easy for them!"

Before she could interrupt, he waved her silent.
"Now that my daughter has decided to leave home,
there are sure going to be some changes made in this
household, you can bet on it."

He stared coldly at his wife, then added, "Before
it's over, them two niggers are going to wish like hell
they had awakened me this morning. I don't give a
fuck what you say, Shirley; I know where I'm coming from. They knew what they were doing when they
watched her load her bags into that cab, and you can
bet on it. Both of them knew damn well I wouldn't
have allowed it, and if they were any kind of brothers they wouldn't have allowed it either!"

When he finished with his outburst, Shirley could
only gaze at him, dumbfounded. She knew he was in
one of his rare moods and prayed silently that it would
pass. Daddy Cool was such a strange man that it was

hard to tell what he might do next. If he felt like it, he would put both of his stepchildren out and turn his back on them completely.

As she watched his departing back, she wondered why her two sons had done what they had done. They both knew that their stepfather would be angry over Janet's departure, and that was the main reason they fled from the house. They didn't want to hear his angry voice when he found out. She remembered how Jimmy had laughed while telling her about Janet's leaving. It had been a joke to him, but now it looked as if the joke might turn bitter.

She didn't believe her boys could make it without her or her husband's help. Neither boy had ever held any kind of job, nor had really taken up anything in school that would help them out. Daddy Cool had bought a car for Buddy on his eighteenth birthday and promised one to Jimmy whenever he graduated from school. But Jimmy had quit in his last year so that he could run the streets with his brother.

After leaving the house, Daddy Cool walked to his car and opened the door. He sat behind the steering wheel for a minute before starting up the motor. He didn't want to go to his poolroom but decided that that would be the best place to get a line on where his daughter had gone.

If only he could catch up with either one of his stepsons, he was sure they would know where she was.

Daddy Cool backed the car out of the driveway. His mind was so occupied with his thoughts that he almost backed into an oncoming car. The sound of the driver's horn warned him just in time.

It took only five minutes before he was pulling into

the rear parking lot of his poolroom. The front of the building advertised the place as "the billiard hall for men and women." A place of leisure. It was not only a poolroom, but catered to other tastes as well. As he let himself in the back door, which was always kept locked, the first thing Daddy Cool did was glance over toward the restaurant section of the hall.

The long counter was empty except for two young girls who were sipping on Cokes as they watched the men in the rear of the place play pool. The restaurant had a long counter plus four heavily padded red booths for people who wanted to eat their food in semi-privacy. The two girls who worked the day shift watched him as he entered. Each one smiled brightly in his direction.

Daddy Cool ignored the waitresses, while his eyes sought out every spot in the place for Janet. The front table that was reserved just for women was empty. Sometimes Janet would spend half a day shooting pool on the women's table.

There were eight tables in the poolroom, but only three of them were in use now. From a high chair that resembled the ones lifeguards used out at the public beaches, the massive Earl sat overlooking his domain. He ran the poolroom the way a captain ran a ship. He didn't allow any foul language on the premises, nor drinking.

DADDY COOL
By DONALD GOINES

Larry Jackson, better known to family and friends as "Daddy Cool," is a black hit man. And his clients know he's the best. He can pull a trigger or toss a knife and never blink an eye. All that counts is the

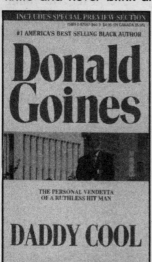

INCLUDES SPECIAL PREVIEW SECTION
ISBN 0-87067-864-3 $4.95 (IN CANADA $5.95)

#1 AMERICA'S BEST SELLING BLACK AUTHOR

Donald Goines

THE PERSONAL VENDETTA
OF A RUTHLESS HIT MAN

DADDY COOL

bread. That and his teenage daughter Janet, whose love means everything to him. He gives her presents and money hoping to buy it. But Janet is taken in by smooth-talking Ronald, a youngblood pimp. He sees Janet as a ripe piece for his stable. He calls Janet's father "Daddy Fool," but Daddy Cool is nobody's fool. When he discovers what the pimp has done to Janet, he acts with a vengeance!